THE QUEST FOR THE
GOLDEN CHALICE

THE QUEST FOR THE GOLDEN CHALICE

Denys S. Sissons

Book Guild Publishing

Sussex, England

First published in Great Britain in 2006 by
The Book Guild
25 High Street
Lewes, East Sussex
BN7 2LU

Typesetting in Palatino by
Keyboard Services, Luton, Bedfordshire

Printed in Great Britain by
CPI Bath

A catalogue record for this book is available from
The British Library

ISBN 1 84624 035 2

CONTENTS

PART ONE

THE FOREST

1

There was no expression on the face of the forest, and no movement among its trees as it lay, silent and still, under the hot sun of midsummer. It was enormous in extent, ranging over hundreds of square kilometres of little-known territory. It clothed the sides of mountains, blanketed entire hills, smothered deep valleys, and spread a dense green mantle of vegetation over all the intervening spaces.

It carried within itself every kind and species of tree, coniferous and deciduous, densely-grouped or loosely-scattered, in every possible shade of green. It harboured all known, and many unknown, varieties of bush, shrub, undergrowth, greenery and plant-life. There were jungles, spinneys, coverts, copses and scrub, impenetrable tangles and bright clearings; lushness and aridity. And in the sunlit glades and the dark thickets there lived and moved every conceivable – and possibly inconceivable – species of animal and insect life, alive and vociferous by day, silent and prowling by night.

Mostly the sun shone from a bright blue sky, and it was hot where the rays penetrated, and cool in the shade. Occasionally great masses of black cloud gathered with ominous deliberation over the mountain and unleashed upon the forest all the awesome splendour and the indiscriminate savagery of a tropical rainstorm. And, as the thunder rolled, the sudden brilliant flashes of lightning illuminated the forest as it was rarely seen: a huge blanket of black sodden vegetation stretching from one horizon to the other, darkly sinister under the torrential rain, undulating and squirming in the violent gusts of wind like some primeval monster of incredible size.

At the moment in time that this story begins, an observer in the sky above the forest would have detected nothing untoward below. The heat rose up from the trees in shimmers and nothing moved.

Then, in a clearing on the southern edge of the great spread of timber, a figure appeared.

It was that of a boy.

He was clad in a brief loincloth, with a leather belt about his waist, and he had rope sandals on his feet.

He had a dishevelled shock of yellow hair, clear blue eyes and a cleft chin.

He was of average height, stocky in build, wiry and agile.

His sole possessions were a skin-bag dangling from his sturdy shoulder, a knife in a sheath fastened to his belt, and a stout staff in his right hand.

His appearance was unremarkable but, as we shall see, appearances can be deceptive.

He looked about him with a puzzled air. Then the look of puzzlement gradually faded, almost as though he had at first not understood why he was there and suddenly the answer had been revealed to him. He gripped the staff tightly and stared around him with an abrupt awareness of his solitude, of his vulnerability, of the possibility that within the dark spaces between the trees there lurked unknown perils. He stood immobile and lifted his head and cocked his ears as might a stag at bay raise its antlered head to listen for enemies. After a long moment, he seemed satisfied that all was well.

'Good!' he murmured to himself. 'And now I must head north.'

Approaching a huge tree, he studied the trunk for signs of mossy growth, knowing that moss always grew on the wet side of trees and that the prevailing wind in that area was westerly. Reassured that his course lay straight ahead, through the forest, he squared his shoulders and set off. The way was easy and he made good progress for the first hour or so. Then his right sandal became loose and he stopped, dropped his bag and staff to the ground, knelt and attended to the refractory footwear.

'Well, hi there!' said a voice directly behind him.

Instantly he leapt up, seized his staff, sprang at least two metres away, spun round and dropped into a defensive crouch.

'My Lord, but we ARE nervous, aren't we?' the newcomer said, looking at him with a smile of amusement.

It was a girl, roughly his age. She had long raven-black hair reaching below her shoulders, dark eyes and a nose ever-so-slightly turned up at the tip. She was clad in a kind of jerkin held together by a belt about her waist, a brief fringed skirt showing her tanned legs, and sandals with crossover laces that encircled her ankles and lower leg. The gap between the lower hem of her jerkin and the top of her skirt showed her flat stomach and revealed that there was a jewel in her navel. Like him, she wore a skin-bag slung from her shoulder but, unlike him, she carried no visible weapon.

It was so obvious that she boded no threat to him that he straightened up, looking – and feeling – somewhat shamefaced.

'I didn't hear you coming,' he said, his instinctive dislike of having to explain his actions adding a slight edge to his words.

She smiled. 'Oh, I can be quiet when I want to be. What's your name?'

For a fleeting moment the puzzled look appeared on his face again, but it cleared almost at once and he answered 'Adam.'

'Oh,' she said cheerfully. 'That means "red earth". Did you know that? You must be from round here.'

She looked at him expectantly. When he didn't say anything, she said 'You're not very friendly, are you? Don't you want to know my name?'

He shrugged. 'What's in a name? I mean, would it do me any good to know what your name is?'

'Yes,' she said at once.

'Why?'

'Because it would.' She waited, but when he didn't reply, she said, 'It's Belle. That means "beautiful". Do you think I'm beautiful?'

Such a question was so outside his limited experience that he ignored it and said, 'Actually, I don't come from round here. But you do, don't you?'

'Yes,' she replied readily. 'I live in the village in the valley over in that direction.' She pointed to the south, then added, 'If you don't come from round here, what are you doing here?'

Once again he looked puzzled for a moment, then his face cleared and he answered, 'I'm here on business. Why, is it a crime to be a stranger in these parts?'

'No, of course not.' She looked at him scornfully. 'What sort of business?'

For a second he had an impulse to be very rude and say 'It's nothing to do with you', but good manners prevailed and he stifled the thought. Instead, he looked about him surreptitiously, then said, 'Can you keep a secret?'

'Oh yes. I'm extremely good at keeping secrets. What is it?'

He said, impressively, 'I'm going into the forest to find Castroglio.'

She stared at him, not in the least impressed.

'You mean Castroglio the so-called sorcerer?'

'Yes.'

She laughed. 'You donkey! There's no such person.'

He became indignant. 'There is too such a person.'

'There isn't.'

'There is.'

'There isn't.'

'There is.'

'Isn't.'

'Is.'

'Isn't.'

'Oh pooh,' he exclaimed, his good manners evaporating. 'You're only a girl. You don't know ANYTHING.'

She looked at him with exasperation. 'But ... Castroglio's only a ... a legend.' Then she added, scornfully, 'You don't REALLY believe he exists, do you?'

'Yes I do,' he said defiantly, now very much on the defensive.

'Alright. WHY do you want to find him?'

7

He opened his mouth to speak, decided not to, and closed it again.

'What's wrong?' she asked sympathetically. 'Cat got your tongue?'

Thus goaded, he replied, 'Alright then, I'll tell you. I take it you've heard of the Sacred Chalice of Saint Anthony?'

Her face sobered and she replied carefully. 'Yes.'

'You know about it?'

'Everyone knows about it.'

He looked round cautiously, then went on, in a low voice. 'They say it's hidden somewhere ... underground ... behind a huge Gate. And there's a Guardian of the Gate to protect the Chalice, and no one has ever got past the Guardian and lived, and no one even knows what it is.' He paused, as though for dramatic effect, then added, 'I'm going to find the Chalice and restore it to its rightful owners.'

The drama didn't work. Her only reaction was one of scornful incredulity.

'You?'

'Little me,' he replied, nettled at her attitude.

'Why?'

'Why?' he repeated. 'Well, because...' He hesitated, then said, a trifle lamely, 'Because I want to, that's why.'

'That's no reason.'

'Yes it is.'

'No it isn't.'

He decided not to enter into the game of verbal pat-ball they had engaged in a few minutes before, and replied, 'Well, alright then. Because it'll make me healthy, wealthy and wise, and that's what I want to be.'

'Aren't you healthy, wealthy and wise now?'

He shook his head, aware that he was on shaky ground and not wishing to take the conversation further. But she was persistent. 'If you're not healthy, what's wrong with you?'

'Oh I'm healthy alright,' he assured her. 'But not wealthy.'

'Nor wise – not if you intend to go on this stupid mission.'

'I'll be a lot wiser when I recover the Chalice.'

'IF you recover it,' she retorted. 'You'll most probably die in the attempt – and then what good will wealth be to you?'

'I don't want the wealth for myself,' he deigned to explain. 'It's ... it's for my parents.' He paused, then added, 'Well, they're not really my parents. They've ... they've taken care of me ever since my real parents died, some years back. But they're very poor and I want them to be rich.'

Her expression was more kindly now.

'But what makes you think you can succeed when so many others have failed?'

'That's why I want to find Castroglio. I believe he has in his possession an amulet that will protect the wearer from evil. I'm going to find him and persuade him to give it me – or, at least, lend it me. And then, armed with it, I can go after the Chalice.'

'You're mad,' she said with quiet conviction. 'Why hasn't anyone else thought about doing the same thing?'

'I don't know,' he said impatiently. 'How should I know?'

'Well, take my advice and think about it. Bless me, Adam, but you really do need that wisdom you're looking for. But you need it NOW – to stop you going off on this hare-brained mission.'

'It isn't hare-brained,' he flared.

'It IS hare-brained.'

'No it isn't.'

'It is.'

'It isn't.'

'It is.'

'Tisn't.'

'Tis.'

'Tisn't.'

'Tis.'

'Oh pooh!' he said. 'I'm going anyway, whatever you say.

'And what about your parents – or whatever they are?'

'They think I'm staying with my aunt.'

'Won't they find out sooner or later?'

'It'll be too late then.'

They stood looking at one another, both at a loss to know what to say next. Then suddenly he said 'Goodbye' and, turning on his heel, plunged recklessly into the forest. She stared at the foliage as it swayed together again after he had passed through, then she shrugged, hitched her bag up onto her shoulder and followed him, but more sedately.

2

Adam strode forward purposefully, his bag swinging at his side, his staff held firmly in his hand. The trees, at first well-spaced, soon grew more densely-packed, and the spaces between the trunks were filled with ferns and briars and thickets, so that he had to slow down to force his way through. The greenery overhead grew thicker and soon blotted out the sun. This was advantageous in that it was cooler in the shade, but it was also much darker and he found himself tripping over roots, plunging into clumps of nettles, and brushing cobwebs and dangling creepers from his face as he progressed.

After roughly an hour of this he decided that it was too much of a good thing this early on in his journey, so halted and looked around for an easier route. In the distance, to his left (and therefore to the west), he saw a patch of sunlight and inferred the presence of a clearing. Hoping that this augured a less difficult path, he altered course and thrust his way through the impeding undergrowth with renewed vigour, eventually – to his relief – breaking out into what was undoubtedly a clearing. And beyond it, on the other side, an indisputable path led away between the trees.

With a sigh of relief he walked out across the clearing...

...and the earth opened and swallowed him up.

For a long moment he sprawled dizzily, not knowing if he was on his head or his heels. Then he realised that he lay at the bottom of a very deep hole. Scrambling to his feet, he rubbed various bruises and looked around him. He was in a circular pit, about two metres across. Staring up, he saw that the mouth of the pit was about four metres above his head. He could see the blue sky, and grass growing round the edge of the hole.

The problem was, how could he get out? The sides of the pit were of tightly-packed earth, vertical and surprisingly smooth, with no crevices that might have done as handholds. He had no rope with him. Gravity being what it was, there was no chance of him jumping out. There appeared to be only one solution: hack out notches for his hands and feet and attempt to climb out. He had only two tools, his staff and his sheath-knife. It had to be the latter. He unsheathed the knife and began to cut away the soil for the first foothold. The earth, although firmly-packed, was dry and easily-worked. He laboriously dug out two handholds and two footholds, then climbed up to make some more. Immediately all the crevices crumbled under his weight and helplessly he slithered back down to the bottom of the pit.

Picking himself up, he moved around the confined space, testing the walls. Finding a spot where the earth appeared firmer, he dug out more cavities and tried to climb up a second time. On this occasion he was more successful and had reached some two metres from the lip of the crater when his supports abruptly collapsed and he fell back to the bottom. He landed awkwardly on his side with a gasping cry that intermingled pain and exasperation in equal measure.

He had just resumed his feet and was rubbing his buttocks and hip ruefully when he heard a voice from above.

'Bless me! What on earth are you doing down there?'

He looked up and saw that the mouth of the pit was partly filled by the head and shoulders of a girl who was gazing down at him.

It was Belle.

'You!' he exclaimed, conscious of a sense of relief.

'Yes, me. What are you doing down there?' she asked innocently.

The question fuelled his exasperation and he retorted, 'Playing marbles.'

'In that case,' she replied casually, 'I'll leave you to your game.' And her head and shoulders disappeared from view.

'Don't go!' he called out, almost in a panic. 'I'm sorry. I was a smart-alec. I fell in. Can you help me out?'

For one agonised moment he thought she had deserted him, but then her head popped back into view, much to his relief.

'Say "please",' she requested.

'Please,' he said, his eagerness to be rescued overcoming his dislike of the indignity thrust upon him.

'That's better. You really must learn to be polite, you know. Politeness costs nothing, yet brings the user rich rewards. Remember that. Have you got a rope in your bag?'

'No.'

'Oh. Then how do you suggest I pull you out?'

He thought hard, then said, 'What about cutting

down some vines or creepers and plaiting them together to make a rope?'

'Good thinking,' she acknowledged, and he felt a warm glow of approbation. 'Throw that knife up I see on your belt.'

Some fifteen minutes later he climbed up the homemade rope out of the pit. He saw that she had fastened the other end of the intertwined creepers to a tree trunk.

'Thanks,' he said breathlessly.

'Don't mench. How did you manage to fall down there?'

'How do I know?' he asked with pardonable irritation. 'I just did.'

'Bless me, you mustn't be so tetchy,' she rebuked him. 'You're far too impatient. Patience is a virtue: remember that. You couldn't have been looking where you were going. Boys!' She said the word with such scorn that he searched in his mind for some way to come back at her. But in the end all he could say was, 'You must have been following me. Why?'

'I wasn't following you,' she replied calmly. 'I just happened to be going the same way as you.'

He looked sceptical.

'I suppose YOU don't want to find Castroglio as well?'

'No. I told you I don't believe he exists. I'm looking for someone who I know DOES exist.'

'Who?'

'My brother Damon.'

'Your brother Damon? Why, where is he?'

'If I knew that I wouldn't be looking for him, would I?' she replied tartly.

'Who's being tetchy now?' he asked triumphantly.

14

She shook her head. 'I'm worried about him. He's gone and got himself lost.'

'Lost? In the forest?'

'It happened about two months ago,' she said. She seemed suddenly glad to be able to tell someone about it. 'He left home to come into the forest – well, that's where he said he was heading. He's very interested in all forms of wildlife, you see. It's his hobby. Not to kill them – he'd never hurt a fly – but to watch them and study their habits.' She paused and her mouth quivered. 'He never came back. We all looked for him: there were search-parties out for weeks afterwards. The Mayor even offered a reward for information. But he was never found.'

'And that was two months ago?'

She nodded, for a moment unable to speak.

'I AM sorry,' he said sincerely. He pondered, then added, 'But what makes you think he's still...' He stopped and could have bitten his tongue as he saw the look of distress on her face deepen.

'Alive, you were going to say,' she said.

'I'm sorry, I didn't mean to...'

'Doesn't matter. Boys are all the same.' She looked at him with an expression of defiance on her face. 'I KNOW he's still alive.'

'How do you know?'

'I just do.'

'How?' he persisted.

'I've ... I've heard from him.'

'Heard from him? How? You mean, by letter?'

'No.' She drew a deep breath. 'If I told you, you wouldn't believe me.'

'Try me.' When she remained silent, he coaxed her.

15

'Come on, tell me. How have you heard from him?'

'In my head.'

'In your...' He stared at her in amazement and she blushed. 'I told you you wouldn't believe me,' she said shortly.

'We-e-ell,' he said slowly, unwilling to antagonise her. 'It wants some believing, you know. How do you mean, in your head?'

'Exactly what I say. I've had messages from him. They come to me inside my head. I've had them several times since he was ... lost. It's the same message each time. He's alive, but imprisoned somewhere. He doesn't know where, but I'm to come into the forest and head north. That's all there is, but it's enough for me. So here I am, on my way. I'm determined to find him. We ... we were very close.'

'Have you told anyone else about these messages?'

'No. They wouldn't believe me, just like you don't.' She looked at him as though daring him to comment, but he didn't speak so she went on. 'Well, I must be off. I have a long way to go. Don't fall down any more holes.'

'Hold on!' A wild idea flashed into his mind, although he wasn't sure why. He deluded himself that it had nothing to do with this girl – this rather strange, very independent, but undeniably pretty girl who had just rescued him from a nasty deep hole, both literally and metaphorically. And yet...

'Sorry, can't stop,' she said. 'Have to be on my way.' And she turned to depart.

'Wait!' he exclaimed. 'Why don't we join forces?'

She stopped in her tracks, remained in thought for perhaps ten seconds, then slowly turned to face him.

'I don't see how we could do that. You're looking for Castroglio and I'm looking for my brother. How can we join forces? If you mean you want to help me look for Damon, that's different. But if you want me to help you look for a non-existent sorcerer, then I've got better things to do.'

'We're both going in the same direction,' he pointed out. 'Why don't we go together – until you find that you've got to go in a different direction from me.'

Again she pondered. Finally she nodded.

'Alright. But I must be free to go my own way when I need to.'

'Let's go then,' was his only reply, and for the second time they set off on their quests, but on this occasion side by side.

3

For several hours they worked their way deeper and deeper into the forest. They took the path that led away from the pit into which Adam had fallen, but it soon petered out and they were once again pushing through thick undergrowth. Occasionally the masses of foliage overhead would break to provide patches of warm sunlight, but mostly the wood was full of dim recesses, dark places, shadows, foetid nooks and crannies. Clouds of flies harassed them from time to time, birds took fright and flew away with loud cries of annoyance at being disturbed, and small and unseen animals scurried away into dense thickets and coppices as they approached.

Eventually they encountered another path and followed it until it crossed with a second track. They paused at the crossroads and looked at one another.

'Which way?' asked Adam, mopping his perspiring brow.

'Straight on,' Belle replied without hesitation.

'Don't I get a vote then?' he asked with slight sarcasm.

'Of course you do,' she replied tartly. 'So which way do you fancy?'

'Straight on,' he said with a grin. She hit him on his arm and he yelped with feigned agony and shot off at full speed along the way ahead. She followed with speed that easily equalled his. They continued in this headlong and reckless manner for several hundred yards, but then came to an abrupt halt as the path forked, passing both sides of a huge and very old tree with a wide and excessively gnarled trunk.

Once again they looked at one another.

'It's an easier choice this time,' said Belle. 'Only two ways to go instead of three.'

'Only three ways instead of four,' he corrected. 'We COULD go back.'

She shook her head and her long black hair waved gracefully in emphasis.

'Oh no we couldn't,' she said positively. 'I'm not going back – EVER – until I find my brother.'

He couldn't think of a satisfactory answer to that, so let his eyes roam round until they alighted on a notice he hadn't seen before. It was no more than a rough board nailed to the tree trunk, and there were words on it, but the board was so worn by wind and weather that they were barely decipherable.

'Look at that,' he said, pointing to the board. 'I wonder what it says.'

'You could perhaps climb up and see,' she suggested.

'I could,' he agreed.

The deeply-gnarled bole offered plenty of footholds and handholds, and within a few seconds he had shinned up it like an active monkey and was reading the notice.

'What does it say?' she called out, looking up at him.

'It doesn't say anything,' he replied. 'Boards can't talk.'

'I mean, what's written on the notice, stupid!' she snapped.

'There's nothing written on the notice: it's printed –

stupid!' he retorted. 'As a matter of fact, it's in rhyme. Listen:

'IF YOU DON'T KNOW
THE RIGHT WAY TO GO
THEN RING THE BELL TWICE
TO GET GOOD ADVICE'

'What bell?' she asked, apparently unimpressed.

'There's one hanging from a branch up here,' he reported. 'Should I ring it?'

'Why not? If we don't, we'll always wonder what would have happened if we had.'

'There's something in what you say,' he agreed. He rang the bell twice, then slid down from his perch. A whole minute passed, then with startling suddenness a door in the tree trunk swung open without a sound and there stepped forth a most peculiar creature.

He was much smaller than they were, but also much older. He was short and fat and wore a faded yellow smock over baggy brown trousers, and green slippers with pointed curly toes. White whiskers spread luxuriantly around his wrinkled face and he was the unfortunate possessor of a very large, very red, and very warty nose. He gazed at them calmly and said, in a husky voice, 'Where d'ye want t'go, huh?'

They both answered at the same time.

'To find Castroglio the sorcerer,' said Adam.

'To find my brother Damon,' said Belle.

'One at a time, one at a time!' remonstrated the other. He took a carved pipe with a hooked stem from an inside pocket and puffed at it. Adam was surprised to see that it was already lit, and wondered why it hadn't

20

burnt a hole in the creature's pocket. The volume of smoke from the pipe increased as the dwarf continued to draw on it, but he evinced no sign of making any further conversation.

'Well?' said Adam, beginning to get impatient.

'Yes, very well, thanks,' nodded the dwarf imperturbably. 'And you?'

'No, no, I mean well, what about telling us which way to go,' snapped Adam, who was a bit highly-strung and didn't tend to suffer fools gladly.

'Depends where you want to end up,' countered the dwarf, still puffing industriously at his pipe.

'We've already told you,' said Adam, controlling his irritability.

'Yes, but you haven't told me your DESTINATION,' replied the dwarf. 'Destinations are very important, you know. I myself am a great believer in destinations.'

'Don't you mean "destiny"?' queried Belle helpfully.

'No, I don't. Destiny is a sort of final destination. I mean ordinary, everyday run-of-the-mill standard-type destinations. How do you feel about them?'

Adam didn't know what to say, but Belle apparently did. 'Some say it's better to travel hopefully than to arrive,' she said brightly.

'Oh, ARRIVE!' said the dwarf with great scorn. 'Anyone can ARRIVE. It doesn't take any great skill to actually ARRIVE. But to reach one's destination ... ah, now that's a wonderful thing to do ... wonderful!'

'Huh!' said Adam, feeling the dwarf was a bit weird but anxious to keep his end up. 'I've arrived at many a destination in my time.'

'Have you! Have you indeed!' said the dwarf eagerly. 'And how did you feel about it? Did you

21

really and honestly enjoy the experience?'

'I suppose I did,' replied Adam, feeling a bit puzzled at the way the conversation was developing.

Belle obviously thought it was developing in quite the wrong way, because she took a small, framed picture from her shoulder-bag and handed it to the dwarf. Adam saw that it was the likeness of a youth perhaps a year or two older than he himself, with a cheerful round face surmounted by a mop of curly black hair.

'This is a picture of my brother Damon,' she said to the dwarf. 'He came into this forest about two months ago and we haven't seen or heard from him since. Have you seen him?'

The dwarf peered at the picture through a thick cloud of smoke. Within seconds his face went as red as his nose had been, his nose grew even more inflamed, and he began to shake all over.

'That ... that PERSON is your ... your brother?' he choked.

'Yes,' said Belle, showing alarm at the other's reaction. 'Why?'

'Why?' repeated the dwarf, now almost apoplectic with choler. 'Why?' his voice rose almost to a shriek. 'I'll tell you why. Because he had the nerve ... the incredible gall ... the unutterable cheek ... the colossal audacity ... the almost unbelievable NECK to ... to...'

To their surprise and alarm he began to swell up, his body inflating in every direction, his smock and trousers growing tighter, his face assuming a smouldering puce colour.

'Quick!' gasped Adam, seizing Belle's hand. 'Let's run!'

Together they ran down the left-hand path, choosing

22

this direction because the furious and now thoroughly-bloated 'dwarf' stood in the centre of the other one. They ran desperately, not looking back until they had negotiated at least half-a-dozen bends and curves, and the thick forest hid the frightening sight of the grossly-swollen dwarf from their view. Then they halted, and leaned against a tree, pumping air into their lungs.

'Bless me, but I was scared!' gasped Belle. 'Do you ... do you think he might have ... burst?'

'He might have,' agreed Adam, panting freely. 'Whatever could your brother have said or done to make him SO mad?'

'Nothing harmful,' said Belle defensively. 'My brother wouldn't hurt a fly if he could help it.'

'Mmm,' murmured Adam, carefully non-committal.

Belle gave him a sharp glance, but he maintained a neutral expression and said, 'We'd better get on – in case he's rolling along after us and wants to explode in our faces!'

'Well, at least I know Damon came this way,' was all she said.

They ran along the track until their breath gave out, then slowed to a walking pace. An hour later they stopped for a quick snack, sharing bread, butter and cheese, with slices of rich fruit cake to follow, and all washed down by copious draughts of ready-brewed lemonade which Belle had brought with her. After the meal they carried on along the same way, hoping to meet someone who might answer their questions sensibly and not swell up with incandescent rage.

Eventually they came to another fork. Both ways

looked equally promising, so Adam produced a coin and it was shields for the left and flowers for the right.

Flowers came up so they took the right fork and pressed onwards.

4

As they made further progress, they became aware that, on their left, the undergrowth had gradually changed into a three-metre high barrier of impenetrable brambles and briars. To their surprise it looked as though it had been cropped, presumably with a scythe, into a definite hedge. As they continued to walk alongside it, the grooming became more evident.

'I reckon there's a garden the other side,' opined Adam. 'That's a real, honest-to-goodness hedge right enough. There could easily be a huge garden behind it – perhaps even a house. If there is, we could knock on the door and ask the way.'

'A house and a garden deep in the forest?' queried Belle, her brow furrowed. 'Seems a bit unlikely to me.'

'Can you think of any other explanation?' he demanded, somewhat exasperated by her scepticism.

'No. Let's carry on. If we come to a gate, then I might believe you.'

They hurried along, eager to see what developed. The hedge continued for perhaps a hundred metres or so in an unbroken line, which was eventually ended by a gap about two metres wide. They walked up to it and cautiously peered inside. Another well-groomed hedge met their gaze. Adam ventured in through the gap. Avenues bounded by the same high impenetrable hedges went away left and right, each terminating in a corner and another hedge.

Belle followed him in and they stood together, staring. 'It's ... it's a maze!' she said at last.

'Amazing!' quipped Adam, but the feeble joke fell flat. She turned a puzzled face to him and said, 'But why here, deep in the forest? It doesn't make any sense.'

'Perhaps it isn't a maze. Perhaps it only looks like one. Stay here.'

He walked along the left-hand avenue until he reached the corner, then peered round. Finally he retraced his steps back to her.

'It carries on, and there are more hedges and corners and avenues. It's a maze alright. Think we ought to try it?'

'What's the point?' objected Belle. 'If it IS a maze, it won't lead anywhere. We don't know if there's anyone inside. We could easily get lost – I'm hopeless in mazes. I think it would be a waste of time when we could be going on and getting somewhere.'

Adam nodded – albeit a trifle reluctantly – and they were about to step out through the gap when she grasped his arm. 'Listen!'

Adam stood still, and faintly to his ears, as though carried by a very small breeze, came a tiny voice.

'Help!'

'Who was...' he began, but she shook him angrily. 'Hush! Listen again.'

'Help!'

This time the cry was slightly louder.

'That came from inside the maze,' Belle said positively. 'Someone's lost in there and can't get out.'

'Help!' It was the distant voice again. 'I'm lost in here and can't get out.'

'We MUST do something,' said Belle, even more positively.

'Like what?' Adam objected. 'You said just now you were hopeless in mazes, and we might easily get lost ourselves, and what good would that do, either for us or whoever's in there?'

'Circumstances alter cases,' said Belle. 'We can't just go away without doing SOMETHING. Whoever's in there might die!'

'Help!' The voice came again. 'You can't just go away without doing something. I might die.'

Adam's brow corrugated. 'The voice keeps repeating what you say,' he said suspiciously. 'It could just be a trap.'

'Not necessarily. Perhaps she can hear us like we can hear her. I say that because I'm sure it's a girl – and I'm not sure it's a trap. Adam, we've GOT to help her.'

He shrugged. 'Okay.' He gripped his staff determinedly. 'Let's go then. Which way?'

'Hold on!' Belle took from her shoulder-bag a large reel of thread and tied one end to a thick branch at the maze entrance. 'Good job I brought my sewing outfit with me. We'll pay this out as we go, then we won't get lost.'

'Very clever,' muttered Adam, sick that he hadn't thought of the idea himself, but slightly consoled by the fact that he didn't own a reel of thread anyway.

'Shall we go?' she said. Adam nodded and together they moved, cautiously and quietly, into the interior of the maze.

By the time they had traversed several dozen avenues

between the hedges, turned left and right many times, and penetrated quite a way into the maze, Adam began to suspect that it was both larger and more complicated than he had at first suspected. He paused for a moment and mopped his brow.

'Not as easy as I thought,' he complained.

'Let's give her a call,' suggested Belle. 'She could be looking for a way out herself and we might miss her. Let's tell her to keep still and keep calling out to us so that we can find our way to her.'

Adam frowned. 'I'm not sure that's a good idea.'

'Why ever not?'

'I don't know. I've just got a funny feeling, that's all.'

'Tummy-ache?' she suggested brightly and not very sympathetically.

'You know what I mean.'

'Well, if that's all you've got to say, I'll give her a call.' Belle raised her voice and shouted, 'We're on our way. Stay where you are and keep calling out.'

Belle's voice echoed among the deep avenues between the hedges and several large black birds flapped noisily away up into the warm sunlit air, deeply indignant at having their siesta interrupted.

'Help!' The voice called, still very faint. 'Help!'

'We don't seem to be getting any nearer,' said Adam, and pointed. 'But it's coming from that direction.' Off they went again, twisting and turning, making instant decisions at each fork or junction, traversing numerous avenues under the hot blue sky. Yet, when the voice called 'Help!' once again, it was as far away as ever.

'Do you honestly think we're getting anywhere?' asked Adam dejectedly.

'No I don't. What's worse, we're nearly at the end of the reel of thread. What do we do then?'

'Go back, I should...'

At that moment the deep warm silence inside the maze was abruptly shattered by an ear-splitting roar. It seemed to come from the other side of the hedge by which they stood. Belle clutched at Adam and they stared at one another, pale with sudden shock. A minute passed, without any repetition of the dreadful noise, then Adam found his voice, but couldn't stop it quivering.

'Wh-what was that? I...'

Immediately the terrifying roar came again, and this time the hedge near them was violently agitated and disturbed, as though something huge and fierce was trying to force its way through to them.

'It's ... it's c-coming through!' babbled Belle. Petrified with fear, they backed away from the bulging hedge, appalled at the realisation that whatever it was must have thick armoured hide to be able to thrust so hard against a briar and bramble hedge like that. Adam looked round in desperation.

'We've got to...' he began, but all at once the roar was repeated and the hedge swayed and shuddered under another vicious and powerful onslaught.

'Hush!' whispered Belle in agony. 'It gets worse when it hears you. Let's try and creep away.'

They trod with extreme caution away from the spot, trying not to breathe and being extra careful to avoid treading on dry twigs on the ground.

'I can't think what it can be...' whispered Adam, but the sound was picked up by the entity beyond the hedge and it answered with an appalling roar. The

29

next moment they heard the heavy clump-clump-clump of huge feet as the creature began to follow them along the other side of the hedge.

Belle slapped Adam's arm and put her finger to her lips with a look of entreaty. He nodded and they went through a gap into an avenue leading away from the unseen predator. So far so good, but at that moment Adam trod on a dry twig which snapped under his foot with a loud crack. At once there came an answering roar, louder still this time, followed by heavy and violent movement towards them.

'Run!' gasped Adam. They ran frantically and without caring which way they went, just as long as they headed away from their pursuer. Belle had dropped the empty reel of thread and they ran without direction or conscious volition, diving into avenues and taking gaps and forks as they came to them.

Suddenly, without any warning, they raced through a gap and found themselves outside the maze. Despite their peril, they halted in blank amazement. Then, giddy with relief at the realisation that they were almost out of danger, they ran again, charging headlong into the thick undergrowth and between the trees, now with only one desire in their minds, to put as much distance between them and the fearful but unseen monster of the maze.

5

When they were completely and utterly out of breath, and felt that they were beyond danger, they stopped for a much-needed rest, slumping down in the shade of a huge tree with a gnarled trunk, against which they leaned their backs. For quite a while neither spoke and, apart from the constant chirruping of innumerable birds and the continual hum of insects, the forest lay as though stunned by the mid-afternoon sun. But at long last Adam broke the silence.

'I wonder what it was,' he said, half to Belle, half to himself.

'Well, I don't suppose we'll ever know now,' she said practically. 'But, whatever it was, it was huge and horrible.'

'How can we be sure?' he protested. 'We never actually saw it. It might have been very pleasant and just wanted a chat.'

'In a pig's eye,' she retorted. 'It didn't sound pleasant or friendly. It kept on roaring horribly and pushing its way through that hedge. If that's your idea of being pleasant, then we'd better split up right now.'

'Well, I don't know,' he said argumentatively. 'Perhaps roaring was all it could do. Perhaps it wanted to see what WE looked like: remember it couldn't see us any more than we could see it. It might even have been as frightened of us as we were of it.'

'Never!' Belle's voice was full of scorn. Then she gave him a look of triumph. 'Then you WERE frightened!'

He realised he'd admitted more than he wanted to. 'A ... a bit,' he conceded.

'Well, I was and I admit it freely. The last time I felt like that was when my little sister fell into the river near our home and nearly drowned.'

'What happened?'

'There was a man standing on the bridge. He saw her as she was swept underneath, dived in and managed to rescue her. Wasn't that lucky?'

'Very. So you've got a sister as well as a brother.'

'Yes, but she's several years younger than me.'

'What does your father do?'

Belle's face fell. 'He's ill in hospital at the moment. He's had a serious operation and is recovering, thank goodness, but it'll be months yet.'

'But what does he do when he's well?'

'He has a shop in the village – a general store. My mum's looking after it for him.' She looked at him. 'You said your parents were dead, didn't you?' He nodded. 'How long ago did they die?'

'My father died about three years ago, my mother some months later.'

'What did your father do?'

He hesitated, then said, 'He was a guard at the Palace.'

'You mean the Palace of the Lord of Moldavia?'

'Yes.'

'They say only the best in the land manage to get to the Palace.'

'So they say. He was a Sector Captain.'

'Bless me, Adam, but you must have been very proud of him. Did he die in combat?'

32

'Er ... yes.'

It was obvious that he was reluctant to talk about it, so she changed the subject. 'Have you any brothers or sisters?'

'No.'

'You're all on your own? And an orphan! Haven't your godparents any children either?'

'No.' He plucked a long blade of grass and began to chew it. 'I suppose that's why they were glad to take me in.' Then his brow furrowed, as though remembering something. 'But I'm not *all* alone. I've got a ... a dog.'

She laughed. 'Not quite the same thing, but...'

At that moment she stopped speaking and stared, open-mouthed, as a small animal appeared in the distance, along the path they had been following.

'Bless me!' she said. 'Look there. It's a dog! How funny!'

As if it heard her – or spotted them both under the tree – it suddenly charged towards them, yelping excitedly.

'Come on, boy!' exclaimed Adam, sitting up joyfully. 'Good boy then!'

The dog raced up to them and went into paroxysms of ecstatic welcome, leaping and treading all over them, licking their hands and faces and giving vent to little yelps of pleasure.

Adam said, 'It's a bit like my own dog, Biscuit, back home.'

Belle said, her eyes glimmering, 'You may have a dog-biscuit back home, but it can't look anything like a dog, surely?'

'Oh, ha-ha! No, I call my dog Biscuit because he's

light brown, with dark brown spots, like a chocolate cookie.'

'Every dog must have its day,' Belle remarked inconsequentially.

This particular dog was pocket-size, of doubtful ancestry – a cross between a terrier and a poodle. It was all-over grubby-white, with black splodges here and there, one over the right eye investing it with a distinctly piratical appearance. It had a very wet nose, as they had by now discovered, and large brown soulful eyes. It wore a collar but no means of identification.

'I wonder what it's doing here in the forest?' said Belle.

It trotted several paces back the way it had come, then twisted round, looked back at them appealingly, and yelped.

'What's the matter with it?' asked Belle.

'I think he's trying to tell us something,' decided Adam.

The dog went on a few paces, then performed the same manoeuvre.

'He wants us to follow him!' said Adam, springing to his feet. As he did so, the dog barked excitedly, revolved several times and then trotted off down the path.

'Come on,' said Adam, holding out his hand. Belle got to her feet and together they ran after the dog, which was now moving faster, every now and then looking back to make sure they were following.

'You don't think this is another trap?' panted Belle as they ran.

'Another trap? What do you mean?'

'Well, if you think about it, the hole you fell into

34

was some kind of trap. And I'm certain those cries for help in the maze were another trap. I'm beginning to think this forest is a very nasty place, with all kinds of traps to keep us from...'

She stopped speaking as they ran after the dog and Adam said, 'Keep us from doing what?'

'...whatever we have to do,' finished Belle lamely.

'I dunno,' he said, partly because he didn't know what to think and partly because he didn't have sufficient breath left to talk with. But he couldn't help thinking to himself that there COULD be a grain of truth in what she said. They carried on running through the trees, across sun-dappled clearings and deeply-shaded areas, avoiding large patches of nettles and thistles, keeping the small white figure of the dog in view, until...

'Oh look!' gasped Belle, pointing forward. They stopped in their tracks, hardly able to believe their eyes. In the centre of an apparently inoffensive clearing was a huge giant of a tree-plant, the great gnarled and misshapen trunk at least a metre wide, and crowned with an enormous dense mass of strangely-shaped leaves, large and fleshy, of a peculiarly sickly purple hue. Pinned against the trunk, with her back to it, was a girl, perhaps two or three years older than Adam. She had long blonde hair and was clad in a short animal-skin, and sandals not unlike Belle's. She was fastened to the trunk by a number of thick green ropes that coiled down from the impenetrable mass of fleshy purple foliage above her head. Her eyes were closed, her chin sunk onto her bosom.

The dog rushed towards her, whining piteously. It pulled up short when it got near to the ropes and backed onto its haunches, barking furiously.

'Oh look!' exclaimed Adam, his face pale with horror.

One of the 'ropes' released its hold on the girl's bare thigh, slithered down with great speed and tried to wrap itself about the dog's middle. Fortunately the animal retreated and managed to evade the green 'rope', which then writhed after its prey and groped for it in a very sinister manner.

'It's ... it's alive!' said Adam, flabbergasted. 'That plant's alive and those ... those things are tentacles!'

'What can we do?' Belle whispered, white with the sudden shock. 'We MUST do something – but what?'

'There's only one thing we can do. Attack! You take my staff: I'll use my knife.'

They rushed up to the bound girl and Belle belaboured the green 'ropes' with the staff, whilst Adam seized one that encircled the girl's slender waist and tried to cut it. To his amazement and revulsion it was rubbery and not only resisted his efforts to sever it but also attempted to squirm away from him. He drew a deep breath and applied all his strength, sawing away at the thick green 'cord' until suddenly he broke through the tough outer skin. Immediately a hideous green ichor oozed out of the deep cut and a fearful stench arose from it. All the 'ropes' quivered, and from the mass of foliage overhead came a weird strangled moan as the wounded limb was swiftly withdrawn.

'Success!' shouted Adam, but his triumph was premature and short-lived, because the next moment TWO tentacles slithered down from above. One wrapped itself round the girl's waist, replacing the damaged limb, whilst the other curled about Adam's upper arm. It felt immensely strong and, despite his struggles, it

36

forced him towards the trunk, just as a third tentacle snaked down towards him.

'Help, Belle, help!' he said huskily. The last 'rope' had already fastened itself round his arm and pinned it to his side, rendering him almost powerless. Belle rushed to his assistance and lashed out at the tentacles with the staff, but this seemed to have no effect on them at all.

'Take my knife and cut them!' said Adam urgently. As the dog continued to rush round the fringe of the struggle, barking excitedly, Belle took the knife from Adam and, dodging a green limb that was groping for her like a long blind worm, attacked the coil about Adam's shoulder. She stabbed the knife into the fleshy rope again and again. The result was encouraging: another inhuman noise came from within the dense greenery above their heads and the wounded limb, green slime exuding from half-a-dozen gashes, quivered and was withdrawn.

Adam managed to tear himself free from the other tentacle binding him. 'The girl's got a knife as well!' he gasped and took the weapon from a sheath attached to the belt round the girl's waist. Belle screamed as several more appendages snaked down from above, and then both she and Adam were enveloped in writhing groping coils, each one attempting to pinion them in helpless bondage.

'Keep your arms free and keep on stabbing!' shouted Adam.

Both he and Belle cut and stabbed at the horrible tentacles again and again, retching as the ghastly green matter oozed and spurted from innumerable wounds. They ducked and dodged and weaved to avoid the slimy clutches of the plant-monster's endless tendrils. But to their gradually increasing horror it was winning the battle. Belle was the first to be rendered immobile, which made Adam fight all the harder, panting with desperation as he saw his companion pulled back against the trunk and turned upside down about two metres from the ground so that her brown legs were waving frantically – until further tentacles bound them to the tree as well. But by now Adam's body and left arm were held fast, and only his right arm remained free as he sought to keep it out of the slimy grasp of the enemy. And all the while the dog pranced and barked and very carefully kept out of the way of the waving tendrils.

Belle gave another scream, and this seemed to jerk the pinned girl from her coma. Her eyes opened and she gazed around her. Seeing Adam engaged in his losing struggle, she spoke.

'I say – boy! You there! Before it captures your arm, feel in the purse at my waist. Take out the bottle you find there. Quickly!'

Adam squirmed round so that he could get at her belt. He opened the purse and took from it a small dark-brown bottle.

'Pour the tincture into the wounds,' said the girl calmly. 'Hurry!'

A fourth creeper coiled about his thighs, pinning him more tightly to the tree. Another tried to grab his arm, but he wrenched it free. Extracting the cork from the bottle with his teeth, he poured a small quantity of the contents into a gaping wound in the limb across his chest. The effect was dramatic. A gurgling squeal came from above and the limb shuddered, released his arm and disappeared up into the foliage overhead. Encouraged, Adam dashed the liquid into more wounds. Green tentacles quivered and snaked back into the darkness above; more unearthly noises came from the same area. The next moment he was free and applying more of the liquid to all the cuts and stab-wounds he could find. More and more of the 'ropes' were withdrawn and soon Belle fell to the ground, gasping with relief at being free. The last limb vanished back up into the tree and a violent agitation of the foliage followed. The girl in the animal-skin stepped away from the trunk, apparently unscathed and surprisingly calm.

'We must leave here instantly,' she said with authority. 'Those wounds will soon heal and then it will try to attack again. Follow me. Here, Custard!'

She turned and ran swiftly along the path into the forest, pursued by the excitedly-yelping dog. Adam helped Belle to her feet.

'Are you alright?' he asked anxiously.

She nodded, and together they ran after the girl.

6

The blonde had departed at such a pace that neither she nor the dog were visible. However, Adam and Belle followed, making the best possible speed in their anxiety to get away from the dreadful plant-monster. Ten minutes later they arrived at a clearing and found the blonde girl sitting on the grass, her back against a fallen tree-trunk, the dog sniffing happily at a clump of bushes nearby.

'You took your time getting here,' she remarked, glancing up at them as she chewed on a stem of grass. There was slight contempt in her eyes, which were a very bright blue.

Adam opened his mouth to make a hasty retort, but Belle forestalled him.

'We've been travelling most of the day,' she said sharply. 'I'm getting tired, and I expect Adam is as well.'

'You're Adam?' said the girl, giving him a swift glance of appraisal.

He nodded. 'And this is Belle,' he said, indicating his companion.

The girl did not reply, but continued to gaze at him. He waited a bit, then asked, 'What's your name?'

'Candice,' was the reply.

'That's a funny name,' commented Belle.

'Not half as funny as yours,' retorted the blonde.

A somewhat awkward silence followed. The girl was very brown, her arms and legs exposed by the brief animal-skin, which left one shoulder bare and reached to the tops of her sun-tanned thighs. She wore rope-sandals on her feet. Adam had been expecting her to thank them for rescuing her, and when she made no move to do so he referred to the matter to jog her memory.

'What was that terrible creature back there?' he asked.

'No idea. I was just resting against the tree when it slid down and attacked me. I had no idea it was up there and no chance to do anything.'

'It means "glowing",' said Belle.

'What does?' asked the blonde, frowning.

'Your name – Candice. It means "glowing". Adam means "red earth", and Belle means "beautiful".'

Candice stared at her, then returned her gaze to Adam as though Belle had not spoken.

'Next thing I knew, I was bound to the tree. Couldn't move a muscle.'

'You were unconscious when we arrived,' he reminded her.

'No I wasn't. I was in a hypno-trance, gathering my strength to break loose. If you hadn't suddenly appeared out of nowhere and wrecked my concentration, I'd have been free in another minute or so.'

Adam was struck dumb at this apparent ingratitude and Belle took the opportunity to retort, 'I wish we hadn't bothered to help you then. And if you want to blame anyone, blame your dog, he made us follow him.'

'He's not as stupid as he looks,' was the blonde's only comment.

'Why do you call him Custard?' asked Adam.

'Because he's such a coward. Didn't you see how he backed away when the tree-monster tried to get at him? He's real scared of anything bigger than a mouse. Aren't you, Custard my pet?'

The dog bounced up to her, wagged its tail furiously and licked her hand.

'Do you live near the forest?' Adam asked her.

'No. In it.'

'A house in the forest!' breathed Belle. 'How lovely!'

'Did I say a house?' enquired Candice with scorn. 'I wouldn't live in a house for all the gold in all the world.'

'Where do you live then?' asked Adam, nettled by her attitude.

'Wherever I fancy. Just at the moment I'm in rather a nice little cave in a hillside not far from here. You can't really beat caves for homes, you know, they're very convenient, warm and dry, no draughts, plenty of room. Of course, a minor snag is that you normally have to get rid of the holding tenants first, but that's never much of a problem as far as I'm concerned.'

'Holding tenants?' Adam queried.

'Yes. The one I'm in now had a family of bears living in it. I had to get rid of them first, and then clean the place up a bit. But after that it was well worthwhile. I shall be sorry to leave.'

'You didn't ... kill them?' Belle asked uneasily.

'I don't kill things unless I have to,' said Candice with cold disdain.

'So where did you get that skin you're wearing?' Adam asked pointedly, hoping to score off her.

'The animal in question was already dead.' Then, as

42

though to change the subject, Candice said, 'Why have you been travelling most of the day?'

Belle explained the purpose of her journey and showed the blonde girl the picture of her brother. Candice studied it, then nodded. 'I've seen him.'

'You have!' Belle exclaimed excitedly. 'Where and when?'

'In the forest. About six or seven weeks back. He was passing through, so he said, and asked me the way.'

'Where to?'

'The abode of Castroglio.'

'Castroglio!' said Adam in amazement. 'How fantastic! That's who I want to see. He does exist then?'

'Castroglio? Yes, of course. Didn't you believe he did? Lots of people don't.'

'Belle was one of them,' Adam couldn't help saying, and was rewarded by a pinch on the buttocks that made him yelp.

'Are you SURE he exists?' Belle asked the blonde girl suspiciously.

'Certain.' Candice looked at Adam. 'Why do you want to see him?'

'I don't want to appear rude, but I consider that to be MY business,' Adam replied, trying hard to rob the words of offence.

'I suppose you're after one of his spells,' said Candice scornfully. 'That's all anyone wants of him, poor old dear.'

'Is that what my brother wanted from him?' Belle asked.

'I don't know. He didn't say. He wasn't very chatty.'

'He USUALLY is,' commented Belle.

'Where is Castroglio's abode?' enquired Adam, sitting down beside Candice. Belle looked at him somewhat expressively, but was not able to meet his eyes so followed suit, finding a place the other side of Adam.

'In the Mountain.'

'The Mountain? Which one?'

'There IS only one Mountain hereabouts. It lies about a day's march from here, northward. Were you thinking of going there?'

'Of course,' replied Adam very positively.

'It's not easy. Oh, the Mountain itself is easy to find, but he doesn't live on it but IN it. Deep in the heart of it, and the way lies through a labyrinth of underground passages and through caverns and chambers in which many known and unknown dangers lurk. If you take my advice, you'll forget the whole thing.'

'Yes, well, we don't think we WILL be taking your advice, thank you very much just the same,' said Belle, speaking almost as scornfully as Candice was wont to do. 'I for one am QUITE determined to find my brother, come what may, and so I shall be going.'

'And I shall be going with you,' confirmed Adam, who was rewarded with a brilliant smile from the younger girl that made him feel a warm glow all over. He realised dimly that the advent of the blonde newcomer had somehow caused Belle and himself to draw closer together.

'You're both stupid,' commented Candice. 'And I'm even more stupid for consenting to go along with you and help look after you.'

'You're prepared to come with us?' asked Belle. Adam said nothing, not knowing whether to feel pleased or otherwise.

44

'You wouldn't get very far without me,' retorted Candice, springing to her feet. 'I can show you the way to the Mountain, and once inside it I can assure you that you'll need all the help you can get.'

'Well ... thanks, anyway,' said Adam awkwardly, deciding that it would be better to accept her offer. 'Shall we go then? I believe it's beginning to get dark.'

'It'll be dark very shortly,' corrected Candice. 'There's absolutely NO point in starting now. We wouldn't get very far, and in any case I need to make a few preparations first. I'll take you back to my cave and we'll have a meal and a good night's sleep and start out fresh in the morning.'

'I reckon that's just wasting valuable time...' began Adam, but the blonde girl ignored him and walked away. The dog yelped excitedly and rushed after her, its tail wagging frantically.

'Well!' said Adam indignantly. 'What about that for arrogance?'

'Don't fret about it, Adam,' said Belle, her hand sliding into his. 'It's only her way. And I really think we could do with her help. Besides which, I AM very tired and I expect you are too, so it IS a good idea to eat and sleep and start out in the morning as good as new. So put away that frown and come along.'

The next day they followed a trail through the forest that was invisible to them, but apparently perfectly obvious to Candice. She was in fact rather like a denizen of the forest herself, with an intimate knowledge of the habits and customs of the various flora and fauna that they encountered (or were likely to encounter) along the way. Whenever they came to a fork, or a junction of paths, she seemed to know instinctively not

45

only which direction to take, but also the directions to avoid. She was able to sense, and consequently skirt around, dangers and perils that she would not or could not explain. She forged steadily ahead, followed closely (or in some cases preceded) by Custard, whose busy little body and waggly tail became a familiar and cheerful sight to Belle and Adam.

By nightfall they had reached the base of the Mountain and, in accordance with Candice's recommendation, slept in a clearing for the night. They were protected by a fire somehow lit by the blonde girl without matches, and gathered their strength and their determination for the following day.

PART TWO

THE MOUNTAIN

1

The Mountain was huge, with a wide solid base. It towered up into the blue sky, rising out of the green blanket of forest like a gargantuan animal rearing up to free itself from its bedding. The thick verdant carpet of mixed deciduous and coniferous trees clung tenaciously to the lower escarpments, but further up it capitulated in the face of the unequal struggle with the altitude and the elements, and thinned down to bush and scrub which gradually merged into tough wiry heather and gorse, finally petering out altogether, leaving the upper slopes bare. The enormous gaunt mass of granite was populated only by eagles and chamoix, plus a varied assortment of the kind of insect life that flourished at such heights and in such rarefied atmospheres.

Towards the summit, the elements claimed victory by depositing and maintaining a thick layer of snow and ice which even in summer never completely left the peak, and in winter extended a good halfway down to the ground. It was at such times – from October through to March – that the upper slopes were frequently ravaged by incredibly fierce storms, during which gale-force winds buffeted the gigantic bulk, and great deluges of hail and snow and icy rain were flung at it from every side. In summer those same storms were accompanied by the same tempestuous winds, but instead of precipitation the heavy atmospheric pressure produced tremendous accumulations of static electricity that unleashed awesome power in ear-splitting thunderclaps, plus vivid flashes of lightning that momentarily lit up the dark mountain and the cowering forest as though it were bright day.

But there were no tempests raging as the three adventurers, plus Custard the dog, stood in a clearing at the base of the Mountain, gazing up at its colossal bulk. The morning was young, the sunshine new and bright, and everything looked serene and cheerful, with no hint nor sign of danger or hostility. They each had a skin-bag slung from the shoulder, Candice had her sheath-knife, and Adam had his knife and staff.

'Bless me, but I don't think I've ever seen such a huge mountain,' said Belle with awe in her voice. 'Surely we don't have to climb it?'

'Pooh, it wouldn't be all that hard,' said Adam nonchalantly, attempting to assert his claim to superiority.

'It jolly well WOULD be hard!' exclaimed Belle.

'It jolly well wouldn't!'

'It would.'

'It wouldn't.'

'It would.'

'Wouldn't.'

'Would.'

'Wouldn't.'

'Would.'

'Great quivering quails!' ejaculated Candice. 'When you two children have QUITE finished with your juvenile bickering, you may remember that I said Castroglio lives IN it, not on it. We don't have to climb it – although I agree with Adam that it wouldn't be too difficult.'

'And we don't have to go round it?'

'No, Adam, we don't. We've got to go inside it. And that means we have to find the entrance. So the sooner we get started the better.'

'Where is the entrance?' queried Belle, as the four of them set off on a journey which would take them round the base of the Mountain.

'I've not the slightest idea,' responded Candice casually.

'How are we going to find it then?'

'It's somewhere on the east side. There ARE markers. I'll find them.'

'What sort of markers?'

'I can't explain. There'll be signs – signs that I'LL be able to interpret, but will not mean anything to you.'

Feeling hurt at what she regarded as a rebuff by the elder girl, Belle said no more but followed the others with some resentment, which soon dispersed under the need to give urgent attention to the way ahead. The forest was especially dense around the base and, in amongst the closely-grouped trees, the impenetrable thickets and the tangled undergrowth, were huge boulders which had rolled down from the slopes of the Mountain and were now covered in matted greenery. Every now and then the bright morning sunlight penetrated the ceiling of intermingled foliage and splashed patches of brilliant light onto the path which, after the comparative dark of the forest, were dazzling to the eyes.

Candice seemed both tireless and ruthless. She forged

ahead with remarkable speed and agility, circum-navigating the many obstacles with such ease and panache that it was clear that she was indeed a real child of the forest, completely at home in what was undoubtedly her natural habitat. The little dog kept up with her without too much difficulty, but both Belle and Adam found it hard going, and sometimes Custard's excited yelping was the only clue to the direction being taken.

After about an hour's strenuous journeying, during which they climbed some way up the lower slopes of the Mountain, they entered an inclined clearing to find Candice sitting on the low branch of a tree, swinging her slim brown legs freely. Custard lay nearby, tongue lolling out, brown eyes looking up at them as though to say, 'Come on, you two, we've been waiting here for ages'. Adam wiped the sweat from his brow and looked belligerently at the blonde as though daring her to say something scornful or derogatory – or both – but she merely glanced at them indifferently and said nothing.

'What's so special about this particular spot?' asked Belle, collapsing onto the grass with relief.

'We've arrived,' Candice announced.

'We have?' exclaimed Adam. He looked about him. 'Where's the entrance then?'

There were more of the huge granite boulders scattered around the clearing. Clearly they had fallen many many years before, because they were all well-nigh hidden by fast-growing foliage such as clinging ivy, climbing creepers and tenacious lichen. Candice pointed to one of them.

'How do you know?' asked Adam reluctantly, as his searching eyes failed to spot a clue.

'Didn't you have ANY education?' asked Candice wearily.

'I was top of my class at school,' retorted Adam indignantly, then added, 'Well … almost. Especially at reading, writing and arithmetic.'

'I don't mean that,' said Candice scornfully. 'I mean the important things in life – things they never teach you in school. For instance, use your eyes and tell me what's different about that boulder from all the others hereabouts?'

Adam studied it intently, but it was Belle who answered. 'Well, it's not covered in leaves and things.'

'Right. Moss – yes. What you call "leaves and things" – no. Why?'

'Because it's newer than the others.' Adam hazarded.

Candice laughed. 'Half-right. Why is it newer than the others?'

'Because it fell down very recently,' said Belle brightly.

'Again, half-right. But it didn't fall. It was placed there.'

'Placed!' exclaimed Adam. 'But … it must weigh a ton or more!'

'All of that. Nevertheless, it was placed there. Why?'

They both thought hard, but it was Belle who came up with the answer.

'To hide the entrance!'

'Right!'

As Adam ran over to the boulder, pursued by Custard with its customary shrill yelps of pleasure, Belle asked, 'How was it placed there?'

'There are ways,' replied Candice with a shrug. The two girls went over to join Adam, who was now as excited as the dog at having discovered a narrow crevice between the boulder and the hillside. 'Is this it?' he asked. Candice nodded. Adam thrust with all his strength at the boulder, but he might as well have heaved at the Mountain itself: the boulder seemed rooted to the ground. 'How does it open?' he asked.

'Watch,' said Candice. She studied the boulder, then set her hands against a craggy projection and pushed. To the amazement of the two onlookers, the boulder moved, swivelling slowly and ponderously on hidden pivots, until the crevice was half a metre wide. Beyond the jagged rim of the aperture it was totally dark and silent.

'This is it?' Adam asked incredulously. Candice nodded. Custard sniffed cautiously at the gap, ears well back, tail motionless; then it gave a small whimper and backed away.

'Look at him!' Candice said with disgust. 'He's such a coward. He won't go inside until I do.'

'And THIS is the way to Castroglio's abode?' queried Belle.

'Well, this is where he USED to live.'

'USED to?' repeated Adam, staring at her. 'You mean you don't know if he still does?'

'I've not heard that he's moved,' Candice replied serenely.

'Well, just supposing he HAS moved,' Adam said indignantly. 'We'll have come ALL this way for nothing.'

'Oh come on, use your brain, boy!' she snapped. 'One: the chances are that he hasn't moved. Two: if he HAS moved he'll no doubt have left some kind of forwarding address. Three: If he hasn't left a forwarding address, someone living nearby may know where he's gone to. And four: have you got any bright suggestions as to what ELSE we might do?'

54

Try as he might, Adam couldn't think of a reply which would adequately cover the points she had made, and in the end he had to be content with saying, a trifle peevishly, 'Well, let's go inside or we'll never get anywhere.'

'Hold on!' said Belle. 'I presume you've both noticed how dark it is in there. How do we find our way?'

'Oh I expect cleverclogs here has a lantern in her bag,' replied Adam with petulant sarcasm.

'No lantern,' responded Candice imperturbably. 'No need for one. It's all been taken care of.'

She unsheathed her knife and cut a stout stick from the undergrowth. Then she picked up the wriggling dog and squeezed through the aperture into the darkness beyond. Adam and Belle followed, then halted as Candice's voice came to their ears.

'Don't move until your eyes become accustomed to the dark.'

They obeyed her, and gradually the intensity of the darkness decreased until they could see each other's outline.

'I say, there's a little light ahead,' said Adam.

'Yes, we have to go in that direction. Follow me – carefully.'

They went in single file towards the light, stumbling along an uneven path between walls of rock. The pinpoint of illumination grew larger, until they saw that it came from a tiny wooden cage hanging on an ancient iron hook projecting from the rockface. As they drew nearer, they saw that it was a small round cage a bit like a miniature birdcage. Inside, on a tiny wooden perch, rested a creature with small fluttery wings and very bright eyes like pinpoints of fire. From it radiated a surprisingly bright green light.

'It's like a large glow-worm!' said Belle as they halted by it.

'Right!' nodded Candice. 'In fact, it's a glow-moth. They use them down here for lanterns. Feed them on honey and they'll go on glowing until Domesday – whenever that is. Let's go inside and get some.'

She pushed open a door they had not seen before, and they followed her into what looked like (and actually was) a small, low-ceilinged shop. There was a counter, empty save for a very old-fashioned pair of scales, and behind the counter were many shelves on which were stacked dozens of cages each containing one glow-moth. Apart from the odd yellow jar scattered about, the cages seemed to be the full extent of the shop's stock. Only one or two glow-moths on each shelf radiated their own weird green light; the rest appeared to be lifeless.

'Oh they're all dead!' Belle exclaimed in dismay.

'Not so,' said someone in a very high-pitched voice.

'Who was that?' asked Adam, staring round him into the gloom.

'Just resting,' said the same high voice. 'Not dead.'

From below and behind the counter rose a strange face, made even more strange by the green radiance from the glow-moths. It was approximately moon-shaped (full moon, that is), with a luxuriant fringe of white whiskers, two bulging eyes, a very small squashed tomato for a nose, and a mouth full of very bad teeth.

'Er ... I'm sorry,' stammered Belle, taken aback by the sudden appearance of this somewhat bizarre countenance.

'They're just resting,' replied the face. 'They can't work all the time, you know. But feed 'em a spoonful

56

of honey and they'll almost blind you with their beastly glowing. I don't like it one bit: hurts my eyes something cruel. So I just keep one or two going on each shelf and then it doesn't get too much for me. Any questions?'

'Er ... no, I don't think so,' said Belle hurriedly, a bit frightened of the shopkeeper – for that's what she assumed the newcomer to be.

'Well, you should have,' remonstrated the moon-face. 'You'll never learn if you don't ask questions.' The face bobbed a bit higher, almost like a balloon taking off. 'It has to be the very best honey, of course: nothing else will do. They're particularly fond of clover honey – that makes 'em work extra hard. A good meal of clover honey and they're fair dazzling for days on end. Any questions?'

'Yes. What makes them give out that funny green light?' asked Adam, anxious to ingratiate himself by appearing eager to learn.

The bulging eyes turned on him with an expression of indignation.

'I'm having a conversation with THIS person, not you,' the shopkeeper pointed out. 'Wait your turn. Any questions?'

'Yes,' said Belle hurriedly, trying to make amends for what seemed to have been a gaffe on Adam's part. She took out of her bag the picture of her brother and showed it to the shopkeeper. 'Have you seen this person?'

The shopkeeper looked at it briefly and then said, 'No. And I'm glad I haven't. What a very evil face! Who is it: some awful criminal escaped from gaol and at large so that he can terrorise the populace? He ought to be found and dealt with – and I'd know JUST how to deal with him.'

'Nothing of the kind,' Belle replied angrily. 'He's my brother and he's missing from home and I'm looking for him. And you shouldn't say things like that about people you don't know!'

'OH fiddle-de-dee,' said the moon-face. 'I haven't got time to waste talking to you. If you want anything, say so. If not, kindly proceed about your business and leave me to mine. Any questions?'

'Yes,' Candice interjected. 'Can we have three lanterns, please.'

She placed three coins on the counter. A fat, wrinkled hand came up from behind the counter and scooped them up. The shopkeeper turned, bobbed over to the shelves and took down three cages, which he placed on the counter. He then took from underneath the counter a jar of honey, opened it, scraped out a portion of the yellow stuff with a wooden spatula, and transferred a third of it to a small porcelain dish hooked onto the inside of each cage. To the amazement of both Belle and Adam, each cage-occupant stirred almost at once, and from each tiny head a pair of minute antennae rose up and quivered. Wings rustled and opened, minute pinpoints of fire appeared as the eyes lit up, and the next moment each glow-moth crept along to its dish and began daintily to absorb the honey. Within minutes the three small bodies began to glow with a luminous green radiance.

'The light comes from little bulbs all over their bellies,' explained Candice as she handed a cage each to the other two and took one herself. 'Thank you, shopkeeper, and goodbye.'

The moon-shaped face sank slowly behind the counter again. Adam wanted to peer over it to see what the rest of the shopkeeper looked like, but the blonde ushered them out of the shop and closed the door.

2

'Which way?' asked Belle as all three held their lanterns high.

'To your right,' replied Candice. She put Custard down, fastened a cord to his collar and allowed him to run ahead, but kept a firm grip on the cord. She set off, and the others followed.

The way led slightly downward, an inclined slope between rugged rock-walls about two metres apart, the roof being about four metres above their heads. The ground under their feet was uneven, but not unduly difficult, and they made good progress for the first half-hour. Then Candice began to slow down and to hold her lantern up higher as she cast anxious looks ahead.

'Anything wrong?' enquired Adam, who was bringing up the rear.

'Coming up to the first hazard,' she called back. Suddenly she stopped and raised her lantern, as did the others. The green light illuminated a giant chasm that yawned blackly beneath their feet. Above it, the cavern walls rose up to form a dome of rock overhead. From the depths of the pit came an extraordinary sound that Adam found hard to classify.

'What's that funny noise?' asked Belle anxiously. Even though she kept her voice lowered, it sounded hollow and strange beneath that granite bowl. 'It's ... it's like jets of steam gushing out of the rock.

'Yes, that's what I'd say it was,' confirmed Adam.

'Not steam,' said Candice quietly. 'Something much worse. Hold your lanterns out over the pit, but for pity's sake don't fall in.'

They obeyed her, their apprehensions roused by the sombre tone of her voice. As they espied the cause of the noise, Belle gave vent to a small scream and clutched Adam's arm, whilst he felt the blood drain from his face. The bottom of the pit, some ten metres or so below them, was covered, to a depth of perhaps half a metre, with what at first glance appeared to be a thick carpet of grey spaghetti, but which proved on further examination to be a densely-packed and inextricably-tangled mass of live snakes.

'The Pit of Snakes,' announced Candice in a solemn voice.

Adam gulped and his voice was hoarse as he said, 'There ... there must be hundreds down there.'

'Thousands, probably,' answered Candice. 'All sizes and all kinds, but every one poisonous. Fall down there and...' She shrugged her shoulders.

'How do we get past them?' quavered Belle.

'There's a narrow ledge hewn out of the rock-face both left and right,' replied the blonde girl. 'Either will take us to the far side.'

'Great! Let's go,' said Adam, sounding more confident than he felt.

'Unfortunately, there's a slight snag,' said Candice. 'Up above, in the darkness of the rock-dome, there lives a Vulgel. It's a huge black-grey bird, with red eyes, a long sharp beak, extremely pointed talons, and huge wings tipped with poisoned barbs. If it is awake, and sees someone on either path, it will probably dive down and attack them, aiming to knock them off into the pit. On the other hand, it may be asleep and will do nothing.'

Belle and Adam looked at her in horror.

'Can we chance it being asleep?' asked Adam slowly.

'If there was only one of us, yes. But not with three of us.'

'Supposing two of us go together, one on the left path and the other on the right?' suggested Adam diffidently.

'The extra noise MAY wake it up and it will then attack one or another of the two. But even if the two make it across, it will attack the third one.'

'So what can we do?' asked Belle, her face pale.

'There's only one thing we can do NOW,' replied Candice. 'And that's find a way of beating it – and quickly!'

Adam extracted from his shoulder-bag a strong catapult and, picking up a stone, fitted it into the sling.

'I'm reckoned to be pretty hot with this,' he said modestly. 'If I could see the beast, I could probably kill it. I never miss.'

'You'll only see it when it swoops down,' said Candice. 'And it only swoops down when it sees someone on the path.'

They looked at one another, and the same terrible thought was in all their minds. Belle voiced it, speaking to Candice.

'One of us two must go along one of the ledges and lure it down so that Adam can kill it.'

'Quite right,' replied the blonde. 'And it is I who will go.'

'Why you?' asked Belle belligerently.

'Because I am older, and stronger, and quicker, and more experienced in this sort of thing than you.'

'That's not fair!' exclaimed Belle hotly. 'You may be older, but how do I know about those other things you mentioned? As for being quicker, I can run a hundred metres in fifteen seconds.'

'On the plains I have outrun gazelles,' said Candice.

'I have often matched my older brother at wrestling,' Belle said defiantly.

'I have beaten a full-grown bear in unarmed combat.'

Belle was silent, not really knowing what to say next, and aware of the niggling suspicion that probably Candice WAS her superior, both in speed and strength.

'We haven't time for a contest,' Adam pointed out. 'But, if you want my opinion, I think it right that Candice should go.'

Without further ado, the blonde girl shouldered her bag, held Custard under one arm, picked up her lantern and set off firmly along the ledge round the wall on their right. Adam crouched, his catapult fully extended and aimed, ready for instant action. Slowly Candice worked her way along the ledge, which was in some places only a third of a metre wide, keeping her eyes ahead and not daring to look down. The tension was so great that Adam found himself holding his breath, whilst Belle was rooted to the spot with apprehension. But nothing happened, and Candice reached the far side safely. She turned and looked back at them, her face a pale blur in the green light from her lantern. They could see the little dog wriggling under her arm.

'It didn't come down,' she said as quietly as she could. 'But the next one...'

Adam and Belle stared at one another in utter dismay and the former felt a deep disquiet.

'You can't do it!' he said desperately.

'What else can we do?' Belle wailed.

'We could try going together...'

'You wouldn't be able to shoot at it properly. You'd miss.'

He opened his mouth to deny this, but couldn't, because he knew she was right. He also realised how much he did not want her to go.

'I don't care,' he said at last, doggedly. 'I can't let you ... Belle!'

But she had already left his side, holding her lantern in one hand and Candice's stick in the other. Before he could pull her back she was on the narrow ledge round the wall to their left, moving slowly along, already out of his reach, hugging the rock-wall and holding her head up high.

'Belle, come back!' he pleaded. 'Belle...'

'No Adam,' he heard her say. 'I can't. If I turned now, I'd fall. Get ready to shoot. And PLEASE ... make sure you don't miss!'

In an agony of fear and doubt he knelt down, catapult at the ready, his hands trembling and his mind in a spin. As she approached the halfway mark, he tensed and tried to control his dreadful trepidation.

'Come on, Belle, you're doing fine,' urged Candice from the far side. 'Carefully does it. Everything's fine. No sign of the...'

Even as she spoke there came from above a giant flapping of wings, accompanied by a series of hoarse, croaking noises, and a huge and hideous black bird – the size of the largest eagle ever imagined – dropped down with sickening speed and vicious deliberation from the black gulf overhead. It was headed straight for Belle. Candice screamed a warning. Adam was so astounded by the sight of the savage creature that he was momentarily paralysed and unable to move. The deadly predator was as Candice had described it: black, with large bulging blood-red eyes alight with feral hostility, a long razor-sharp beak and wickedly-hooked talons; and along the black scaly wings were rows of sharp hooks dripping with venom.

Like a stone it dropped, and dived with lightning speed at Belle, who looked up, stared straight into its glaring crimson orbs and shrieked, teetering precariously on the very edge of the narrow pathway.

'Adam!' screamed Candice.

Galvanised into sudden activity, Adam took instant aim and, with a prayer on his lips, loosed off the stone. The missile sped with unerring accuracy, straight as an arrow, crashing into the black body with tremendous velocity and force. The bird gave a hoarse croaking screech, feathers flew, blood sprayed out, and it dropped down into the pit. There was a thud as it landed among the snakes, and the whole tangled mass boiled up into furious hissing activity and engulfed the still-struggling body in only a few seconds.

Candice and Adam reached Belle at the same moment, seized hold of her as she teetered on the lip of the pit and guided her along the remainder of the ledge to the safety of the far side. Here all three collapsed, slumping against the rock-walls to recover, whilst the dog leapt around and over them with ecstatic pleasure, licking everyone and everything indiscriminately. Once they had regained their composure, they talked about the terrible bird and the narrow escape Belle had had. Candice congratulated her on her bravery and Adam on his marksmanship. They took the opportunity of a quick snack and, despite the fact that Belle had borne most of the danger, she soon returned to something approaching normality.

'Are we likely to encounter any more problems like that?' Adam asked Candice.

'We must be prepared for anything,' the blonde girl replied. 'We still have quite a distance to go and not all the perils along the way are known. But if we meet all dangers as well as we met the last one, we shall get through safely.'

'Forewarned is fore-armed,' said Belle.

'Well. I only hope that we're going in the right direction,' muttered Adam, his voice muffled by a sandwich. 'I wouldn't like to think we are going through all this without reaching our objective.'

'Oh, I'm sure we're on the right road,' said Candice confidently.

'I KNOW we are,' said Belle.

'How do you know?' Adam asked. When she couldn't look him in the eye, he groaned. 'Oh, you haven't had another message, have you?'

'Yes,' she admitted, and blushed.

'What's all this about?' asked Candice curiously.

Adam told her about Belle receiving messages in her head from her brother, which made Candice look sceptical and Belle defiant.

'It's TRUE! I don't know how or why. But, last night, in my dreams, I saw him. He was a prisoner in a sort of cage, somewhere below ground. He smiled at me and told me I was getting nearer.'

'You're sure it wasn't just a dream and nothing more?' asked Candice.

'I'm certain,' Belle said shortly.

'How can you be certain?' Adam persisted, but she refused to answer, so they let the matter drop and went on their way.

The path continued downwards and the rock-walls became shiny, with moisture glistening in the light from the lanterns and trickling down in shimmering rivulets. The way grew more difficult and began to twist and turn and change shape, slope and direction. The walls sometimes closed in, whilst the roof receded into blackness overhead, and they had to squeeze through narrow clefts barely a third of a metre wide.

'Good thing not one of us is fat,' puffed Adam as he forced his body through a gap which both the girls – and Custard – had negotiated with ease.

'You mean a good thing at least two of us are not fat,' retorted Belle, looking back at his efforts. 'If the way gets any narrower, we'll be forced to leave you behind. Tubby!'

'I am NOT tubby!'

'You are too tubby.'

'No I'm not.'

'Yes you are.'

'I'm not.'

'You are.'

'Not.'

'Are.'

'Not.'

'Are.'

'Children, children!' rebuked Candice from the leading

position. 'Save your breath for the way ahead. We've a great deal of ground to cover yet.'

'Who does she think she is?' Belle whispered to Adam, dropping back so that the blonde could not hear her. 'Children indeed! She's not that much older than we are.'

'Oh, she's alright,' replied Adam with infuriating tolerance. 'After all, we wouldn't have got very far without her.'

Belle gave him a look of distaste. 'You're not going all sloppy over her, are you?'

'No of course not!' retorted Adam, going pink. 'What rubbish!'

'It's not rubbish,' said Belle. 'Your face was all moony just then.'

Adam was so indignant that he lost his tongue, and Belle turned away the next moment and hurried after Candice.

Not long after that conversation, the blonde girl came to an abrupt halt, so suddenly that Belle cannoned into her and Adam had to put his brakes on very quickly to avoid bumping into Belle.

'What's the trouble now?' he asked peevishly.

Candice stooped and picked up the dog. 'Look!'

She raised her lantern and they saw that the narrow way ahead opened up into a large chamber. Then Belle screamed, and Adam gasped, as the green light shone on a large, thick web that stretched over the entrance to the chamber, reaching from side to side and from ceiling to floor. The stuff of which the web was constructed was coarse and hairy, like very strong grey wool. Apart from the odd remnant of dead fly here and there, it was empty.

'Spider?' asked Adam.

'Worse. That is the web of the Red Skull spider. I wonder where it is? For heaven's sake keep your eyes open and look around with great care.'

'Oh-oh. I wish I hadn't come!' wailed Belle, her voice quivering with incipient panic. 'I LOATHE spiders, even little ones.'

'Well, I have to tell you this is no little one,' warned Candice. 'The adults are about the size of saucers.'

'Why is it called the Red Skull spider?' asked Adam, peering round. He wasn't going to say so, but in point of fact he wasn't ALL that keen on spiders himself.

'Because each adult has markings on its back that look a bit like a red skull. It's nature's way of warning the spider's enemies to keep clear: it is deadly poisonous. One bite, and you are lucky if you die quickly. Adam, get your catapult ready: we may need your expertise in a hurry if it appears. And be prepared: it can move very fast.'

A thorough examination of their surroundings convinced them that it was not their side of the web.

'It could be lurking just round that corner – on either side,' said Candice. It was obvious she was treating the unseen arachnid as a deadly danger, to be approached with the utmost caution. She put the dog down, then handed the other end of the cord to Belle. She took her stick from the younger girl and carefully poked it at the thick threads of the web on their left. The watchers tensed for action, but nothing happened. She did the same thing with the other side, but again there was no result.

'I wonder if it's gone away to hunt for food?' Candice

mused, almost to herself. She stepped forward boldly and lashed at the web with the stick, but the strands were like tough cords and resisted her efforts. Furthermore, they were coated with a thick, gummy substance and her stick caught on the web and she couldn't pull it free. She moved up to the web in order to wrench her weapon away from the adhesive strands and it was then that Belle screamed 'There it is – top right!'

A huge black hairy monster of a spider, the skull-like markings clearly visible on its hirsute humped back, ran swiftly from a dark corner down the strands of the web. Two green eyes shone like iridescent jewels as it headed for Candice, who let go of the stick and stepped back so rapidly that she cannoned into Belle. There was utter confusion for a moment and Adam took the opportunity to loose off a stone, but the spider was moving too swiftly and he missed. The next second the hairy black creature dropped to the ground and scuttled towards them with deadly intent. Belle screamed in total panic and dropped the dog's lead. At the same time, Candice's bag slipped off her shoulder, the strap somehow became entangled in her legs, and she fell sideways. Adam shouted in horror as the spider darted towards the blonde girl's sprawling legs, but the next moment Custard had sprung forward, dragging his lead with him, and pranced at the spider, barking furiously. The spider stopped dead in its tracks and the gleaming green eyes surveyed its new enemy. Adam chose another stone, but he had no time to fit it into his catapult so hurled it with all his strength at the spider – but missed again. As Candice tried to scramble away, the spider ran towards her, aiming straight for her legs. Custard rushed forward, pounced on the black horror, seized its back legs in its teeth and shook it from side to side as though it were a rat.

'No, Custard, no!' cried Candice, more concerned for her pet than for herself. At this juncture Belle picked up Adam's staff, which he had rested against the rock-wall, and lashed out at the swinging spider. She caught it fair and square, missing the dog by a couple of millimetres. The black hairy body was flung against the rock and fell to the ground. Quickly it righted itself and, to the onlookers' amazement, began to crawl towards them despite being hideously wounded, its green eyes blazing with undisguised venom. Belle dealt it another tremendous blow, which stretched it out in what appeared to be a lifeless heap. They watched it warily and noticed the crumpled limbs jerking and quivering now and then. But eventually these spasmodic twitches ended and the creature was, at last, unmistakably dead.

Candice climbed to her feet and the three of them stared ashen-faced at one another. Then she picked up the dog and cradled it in her arms, hugging it and cooing to it as it feverishly licked her face.

'Oh Custard!' she cried. 'I'll never EVER call you a coward again!' She beamed at the other two, her face suffused with pleasure. 'Did you see what this brave little dog did?'

'Yes indeed,' confirmed Adam. 'Good dog, Custard!' He ruffled the fur on the dog's head and it licked him. Then Adam turned to Belle, who was still white as a sheet and trembling with reaction.

'You ... you killed it!' he said wonderingly. 'You hate spiders, yet you killed it.'

'I did, didn't I?' replied Belle faintly. Then she closed her eyes, slid more or less gracefully down to the ground, and lay unconscious.

3

Half-an-hour later they set off once more. By then Belle had recovered from her brief faint, which had been brought about by reaction more than anything else. They had also taken the opportunity to rest and drink before continuing their journey. And now they were on their way again and Candice kept Custard on the cord as she led the way from the chamber. The tunnel sloped downward as it had done before, but the gradient was at first quite gradual. Then, later, it grew steeper and they were obliged to dig in their heels and grab hold of projections and crevices in the walls to stop themselves from sliding headlong into darkness.

When Candice had fallen during the battle with the spider, she had dropped her lantern and, when they recovered it, they found it broken and the poor little glow-moth lying on its back with its thin little legs up in the air. Moreover, no amount of honey – even the very best kind – seemed to have any effect, and Candice had pronounced it deceased. They had therefore started off again with only two lanterns, which made progress just that little bit more difficult.

It may have been lack of sufficient illumination that was responsible for their next calamity. The ground suddenly disappeared from under their feet and they fell like stones. Fortunately they did not fall far, and they landed on a soft surface. As they lay sprawled in a heap and gasping with the shock, Custard bounced up and rushed at his mistress, yelping with pleasure, clearly thinking it was all one great game. The lanterns survived the fall: Adam managed to hold onto his, whilst Belle dropped hers, but it fell on soft ground and remained alight. They scrambled to their feet and raised up the lanterns, to reveal tunnels leading off left and right into impenetrable blackness, and a thick bed of straw under a yawning hole.

'Nice of them to give us something soft to fall on,' commented Candice dryly. 'But they would have done better to warn us that the hole was there.'

'Are you two girls alright?' asked Adam.

'I bumped my elbow, that's all,' said Belle, rubbing the affected part.

'My bottom's a bit sore,' said Candice ruefully. 'I think they skimped on the straw where I fell.' And she rubbed HER affected part.

'Which way now?' enquired Adam, looking in both directions. Custard barked as though in answer. Candice picked up the dog's cord and the three of them looked perplexed.

'I reckon one way's as good as another,' said Belle.

'Toss a coin,' suggested Adam.

'I've got a better idea,' said Candice. 'Let's leave it to Custard.'

'How's HE going to tell us?' demanded Adam. 'He hasn't shown himself to be a brilliant conversationalist up till now.'

Candice ignored the sarcasm. 'All I have to do is put him down and say "Fetch it, Custard!" Whichever way he runs, that's the way we go. Agreed?'

'Yes,' said Belle eagerly.

74

Adam shrugged. 'As good a method as any, I suppose,' he said grumpily, half-wishing he'd thought of the idea himself.

Candice set the dog down at her feet and spoke the magic words. Immediately Custard yelped excitedly and sped away down the tunnel to their left. Fortunately Candice retained a firm hold on the cord and the poor dog nearly strangled itself as it was brought up short.

'Off we go,' said the blonde cheerfully and, holding aloft the lantern which she had taken over from Belle, set off down the tunnel. Belle followed and Adam brought up the rear with the second lantern.

The way twisted and turned, descended and ascended. Every now and then they passed an opening into either another tunnel or a small chamber, but after a short discussion at the first one they agreed to ignore all diversions and continue along the main route.

After about an hour's steady progress, they turned a sharp corner and then halted in dismay. Raising their lanterns, they saw that the path was blocked by a solid wall of rock.

'Oh gosh!' said Belle anxiously. 'What do we do NOW?'

'Turn back, I should think, and take one of those other tunnels we've passed,' suggested Adam, but to his slight annoyance Belle turned to the blonde girl and said, 'What do YOU think, Candice?'

'I don't like turning back,' she said with a frown, and lifted her lantern high up to scrutinise the rock-face. Staring up into the darkness, she said, 'I don't believe this is a dead end. If you look up there, you'll see the tunnel roof goes up as well. I think there's a ledge up there, and it probably continues on at a higher level.'

75

'Fat lot of good that'll do us,' said Adam grumpily. 'We can't climb up there.'

'It wouldn't be easy,' agreed Candice calmly.

'Oh bless me, I don't think I could climb up there,' said Belle. 'I'd be bound to fall and then you'd have to leave me and I'd never be found again.'

'All the more reason for doing what I suggested,' Adam said with satisfaction.

After a moment's hesitation, Candice nodded. 'Let's go,' she said peremptorily and set off back the way they had come. Belle and Adam exchanged eloquent glances – Belle chuckled and Adam's frown melted into a grin as they followed their leader.

But even as they rounded the bend, they cannoned into her. She was standing still, holding tightly to Custard's lead, and listening intently. Belle bumped into her and Adam collided with Belle.

'What's the hold-up NOW?' asked Adam testily.

'Hush!' hissed Candice. 'Listen!'

They stood perfectly still and quiet, their ears cocked. Apart from a faint drip, drip, drip of water coming from somewhere, it was as silent as a tomb. Adam waited perhaps twenty seconds, then began to say, 'I can't hear a . . .' He stopped as an unusual sound came to his ears – a sound, moreover, that caused him to feel very uneasy, although he was quite unable to place it.

'I heard it then!' exclaimed Belle. 'But what is it?'

'Hush!' said Candice again, and this time there was an expression of deep worry on her face.

They waited, tensed, their breathing stilled and their hearts beating. The sound came again, and this time it was louder. They looked at one another with expressions that reminded Adam of a poem he'd learnt at school, in which stout Cortez stared at the Pacific Ocean, and all his men 'looked at each other with a wild surmise'.

'What on earth is it?' he asked, frustrated at being unable to recognise the sound for what it was.

'Sounds a bit like a lion roaring, far off,' confessed Belle.

'Far off, yes,' said Candice quietly. 'But coming nearer. And emphatically not a lion. Something FAR worse.'

'Worse?' ejaculated Adam. 'Like what?'

'Would you believe ... a dragon?'

'A dragon?' he repeated. 'Down here?'

Candice nodded, her face pale. 'I have heard that there is a colony down here. Their lair lies deep inside the Mountain. But they are known to come out seeking food. And we are food to them! The only problem is – is it between us and our nearest escape route?'

'Well, we can't go back and climb that rock-face,' pointed out Adam reasonably, trying to hide the very real feeling of alarm that now invaded his heart.

'We may have to consider doing just that,' Candice said. 'But let's try this way first – but very very cautiously.'

They moved slowly and with trepidation along the shadowy tunnel, every nerve stretched to breaking point, ears cocked for that sound again. And, when it came, Belle gasped and cried, 'Oh, it's EVER so much nearer us! What shall we do?'

'Let's pray we find one of those tunnels first,' said Candice.

A further five minutes passed as they trod carefully along, then suddenly Belle gave a shriek. 'There's an opening, along on the left!'

'For Pete's sake don't scream like that!' expostulated Adam. 'You'll bring the dragon on our trail.'

'I'm afraid he's on our trail already,' said Candice grimly. 'I'd say he's got our scent and is heading this way at full speed.'

As though by way of confirmation, the roar came again, and this time it was terrifyingly near. Belle clutched at Adam and Candice swept the dog up into her arms. 'The question is, which way?' she gritted. 'Ahead, or...'

Once again it was as though the monster had heard her, because there issued another roar, ear-splitting in its volume and spine-chilling in its proximity. The next instant, to their horror, a lick of red flame, accompanied by smoke, erupted from the opening and seared across the rock-tunnel to the opposite wall.

'Bellowing badgers!' gasped Candice, in a tone of such comical dismay that it would have been funny in any other circumstances. 'He's in that side tunnel and we can't get past that flame to go straight ahead. We'll have to go back.'

'To the rock-wall?' exclaimed Adam. 'We'll be trapped!'

'We'll either be burnt to cinders or eaten alive if we don't,' snapped Candice. 'Quickly now!'

Holding the dog firmly, she turned and ran back the way they had come, Belle and Adam following her. Discretion was thrown to the winds as they raced at breakneck speed along the tunnel, and their flight was accelerated by unmistakable sounds of pursuit: the flop, flop, flop of huge feet on the ground, the grotesque flap, flap, flap of large, scaly wings, and an oft-repeated roar interspersed by ghastly snorts and snufflings and hisses. They swerved round the corner and tore on until they reached the rock-face, where they were forced to halt and lean against it, gasping for breath.

'Adam, get your catapult ready,' panted Candice. 'It may not be lethal, but it's better than nothing at all. Use the largest stone you can find.'

Adam selected a sizeable and very jagged lump of rock, fitted it into his catapult pouch with trembling fingers, and waited.

'I can't possibly climb this wall,' said Belle, her voice unsteady. 'We're done for. Oh, I wish...'

She broke off and screamed as flames licked from the corner, smoke belched forth, and with a monstrous flapping of giant wings and another awesome roar, the dragon appeared.

It was about the size of a rhinoceros, but longer. The upper part of the body was covered in a thick, scaly grey hide, whilst the tail was at least five metres in length and equally scaly. In addition, a line of raised spikes, dark red in hue, ran along the back and to the end of the tail. The legs were short and powerful, and terminated in massive feet with seven or eight claws on each. Two strong wings projected from the sides, rather like the stumpy sails of a windmill, each one composed of thick black skin stretched tightly over a skeleton of thin, articulated bones. The head was a fearsome sight: large, with long out-thrust jaws and a snout like a crocodile, equipped with a set of viciously-sharp teeth. The eyes were huge and green, flecked with red, and set at the top of its corrugated head. As it blundered around the corner, flapping its wings, it opened its jaws and emitted another blast of flame and hot smoke, the effects of which reached them a few seconds afterwards. It stopped on seeing them and stood on its four squat legs, its scaly sides heaving, the eyes bulging from their sockets.

'Well, thank goodness it's not an adult one,' muttered Candice.

Adam, trying hard to act as if he wasn't scared, found his voice. 'Not ... not an ... an adult?' he stammered.

'No. They're much bigger and more fierce than this one – especially when they're on the hunt for food. I'd say this one was only about a hundred years old – equivalent in human terms to around eight or nine years.

'You mean he's not dangerous?' asked Belle huskily.

'Oh I didn't say that. He could be as fierce as an adult if he's hungry. But I don't think he is – he looks well fed. But he may still want to play with us, much like a cat with a mouse.'

'But cats kill mice,' quavered Belle.

'Exactly.'

'So what do we...' began Adam, but he was interrupted by Belle, who cried out 'He's attacking!'

Sure enough, the creature gave another roar and lumbered forward, snorting jets of steam and smoke. Adam took rapid aim and loosed off his catapult. The jagged rock hit the dragon on its head, but only bounced off harmlessly.

'No good!' exclaimed Candice. 'It's got a cranium like a suit of armour. Aim for its eyes.'

Adam seized another large stone and fired it. This was a good shot and the dragon gave a hoarse bellow and stopped short, shaking its head from side to side. But the next moment it started forward again, and was now only about thirty metres from them.

'Quick – another shot at the eyes!' shouted Candice.

'I can't find any more stones,' gasped Adam. 'Isn't there anything else you can do?'

Candice pulled her knife from its sheath, set her chin resolutely, and moved towards the dragon. Belle caught at her arm.

'No ... no ... oh please don't!' she cried. 'You'll be killed...'

'I must,' gritted Candice and went forward again. At that moment Adam felt something hit the back of his head. He looked round irritably, then stared in disbelief at a knotted rope that hung down the blank rock-face, swinging gently. He looked up, but could see only darkness above. Almost by instinct he grabbed the rope and hauled on it. It held fast.

'Look, look!' he yelled to the others. 'It's a rope!'

The two girls wheeled round, saw the rope and ran to join him. Candice pulled on the rope just as Adam had done. 'It's our only chance,' she snapped. 'Up you go, you two – and hurry!'

'A stitch in time saves nine,' muttered Belle. Adam pushed her and she grasped the knotted rope and pulled herself up, her slim white legs twisted round the rope as she went up.

'Now you, Adam,' said Candice, her eyes fixed on the snorting dragon.

'No, you first,' he retorted, remembering what his father had taught him before he died. ('Remember, Adam: when danger threatens, look after the women and children. The strong must always protect the weak.') He wasn't sure about Candice being weaker than him, but she WAS female – indubitably so – and therefore entitled to the same treatment.

81

'Don't be silly,' snapped the blonde girl. 'Up you go and NO arguments. Quickly, or I won't be able to make it.'

Adam hesitated, but she slapped his bottom and, flushed with anger, he hooked his lantern onto his belt, leapt onto the rope and climbed up after Belle. The dragon was now very near, roaring madly and belching forth long streamers of flame in frustration as it saw its quarry vanishing. Candice picked up the dog, thrust it into her bag, hitched her lantern onto her belt and made a huge leap upwards, just as the dragon reached the rock-face. If she had missed the rope, she would have fallen back into the dragon's gaping jaws. But her desperately-reaching hands caught the rope, held it, and she pulled herself up, lifting her brown legs just out of reach of the dragon's snapping teeth. The dragon belched out more flames and smoke in furious defeat and Candice felt the heat scorch her lower legs and feet. It roared again and reared up at her, but by now she was climbing rapidly, and experienced a wave of relief as she glanced down and saw that she was now out of harm's way, although she wasn't too pleased at the stench of burning sandals that reached her nostrils. She slowed down to adjust to the slower pace of the two climbers above her, but by now she was well out of danger (provided she didn't slip) and she ascended at her leisure, listening to the sounds from below as the dragon roared impotently, belched out frustrated flames, and flapped its wings in vain.

4

Eventually they reached the top of the rock-face, hauled themselves over the edge, and sprawled on the ground, their limbs aching and their lungs heaving for breath. When they had somewhat recovered, they unhooked their lanterns from their belts and raised them up, thus revealing that they occupied not merely a ledge but a flat platform of rock with several tunnels leading from it. They further saw that the rope that they had climbed, and which had saved them from a very nasty fate, had its upper end tied to an iron ring embedded in the rock.

'Thank goodness we can go on from here,' said Adam with relief. 'I thought we might be stuck and would have to wait until the dragon went off for its tea.'

'I thought WE were going to be its tea,' shuddered Belle.

'But who threw the rope down to us?' puzzled Candice, examining the iron ring. 'Someone must have done.'

'Yes, who indeed?' asked Adam, peering about him. The lanterns were not as bright as they had been (clearly the supply of honey was dwindling) and the remaining light was not sufficient to drive the black shadows from the tunnels leading away from the platform.

Belle was looking about her with a fearful air. 'I have an uneasy feeling we're being watched,' she whispered.

'Who by?' asked Adam.

'How should I know?' she retorted, the terseness of her reply indicating her perturbation.

'I also have that feeling,' nodded Candice, as a result of which all three strained their eyes to search their immediate surroundings.

'Oh bless me, look there!' said Belle, pointing. They saw a group of pale countenances peeping at them from around the edge of one of the tunnels. Adam raised his lantern higher and at once the countenances disappeared. He lowered the lantern and they re-appeared.

Candice laughed and Adam looked at her with surprise.

'Who – or what – are they?' he asked her. 'A bit shy, whoever.'

'Not shy,' corrected Candice. 'It's merely that they can't stand the light. If you mask your lantern, they may come out of hiding.'

Adam covered his lantern with a folded handkerchief, and Candice made encouraging noises and beckoned with her finger. At first there was no reaction, but at last one of them shuffled out of the tunnel, hiding its face behind a crooked arm. Belle gasped. It was short – about a metre in height – and squat, covered in dense grey hair. It had short, stumpy legs and long arms, the hands almost reaching the floor. It had no neck, and the head was like a furry coconut, with not two, but three eyes buried deep in hairy sockets, two in the normal position (with transparent membranes over them) and a third one – without any covering – between them and higher up in the forehead. There was no nose, only two small apertures below the eyes. Further down there was another lipless aperture from which emerged a strange whining chatter.

'What on earth are they?' asked Belle, her eyes wide in amazement.

'Not ON earth, but UNDER it,' replied Candice. 'They're troglodytes.'

She made more chirping noises with her lips, and her hands described inviting gestures. Her efforts were rewarded as two more shuffled out of the darkness. They looked exactly the same as the first one and there seemed to be no way of telling what sex or species they were.

'Troglodytes?' repeated Belle.

'Cave-dwellers. This is a subterranean tribe, never straying far from their homes deep inside the Mountain: that's why they don't like light of any kind. Their third eye enables them to see in pitch darkness. They never go anywhere near the surface, not even on the darkest night. For one thing, their breathing apparatus is not geared for it.'

'Will they harm us?' wondered Belle.

'Good gracious no. They're far more frightened of us than we are of them.'

Two more of the creatures, looking like duplicates of the first three, ventured out and the group stood, hiding their eyes; their small bodies cringed and they were clearly only too ready to dart back into the dark.

'They remind me a little of chimpanzees,' said Adam.

'Yes they would. They're quite closely related to the lower primates – like monkeys, apes, chimpanzees – and they're very timid. They can't talk, either, although some of them may understand simple words. But they have a language of their own, as you can hear.'

'You DO know an awful lot, Candice,' said Belle, torn between admiration and envy. 'Where did you learn it all from?'

'Mostly from a wise old man who lived in the forest,' the blonde girl replied, obviously pleased by Belle's comment. 'He was dying, and I looked after him for several months, and in that time he taught me almost everything he knew.' She carried on chirping and beckoning invitingly, but no more of the troglodytes emerged from the dark tunnel, and in fact the five who had reluctantly ventured out seemed very unhappy and ready to scamper back to rejoin their fellows. Candice imitated their inhuman chattering whine and at the end of it pronounced the name 'Castroglio'. This produced a surprisingly animated response: the coconut heads swivelled, the long hairy arms semaphored, and a burst of the weird incoherent mutterings came from all five in unison. Candice listened patiently, then repeated the name 'Castroglio' several times in a questioning tone. After a further bout of chattering, the hirsute arms were raised again, this time pointing towards one of the tunnels.

'They know of him,' Candice informed the others. 'They say he lives not too far from here. I think we should go now; we won't get anything more out of them and our lanterns are hurting their eyes.'

'Shall I go first for a change?' asked Adam hopefully.

'If you wish,' replied Candice in an indifferent tone.

'What about thanking them for helping us to escape from the dragon?' asked Belle as they prepared to depart.

'They don't understand gratitude,' Candice replied simply.

86

Adam went forward, a little piqued by the blonde's cool reception of his offer. As he raised his lantern, the troglodytes hid their eyes, whined pathetically, then retreated into their own black tunnel and quickly vanished from view. Suddenly he felt a wave of pity for them and the strange subterranean existence to which an apparently unfeeling nature had condemned them. They would never see the sun, never feel the breeze on their face, never breathe cool fresh air.

But he soon forgot the problems and troubles of other species as he faced the dangers and worries ahead. The tunnel led upwards now, quite steeply, and the three of them (plus the dog) toiled up the slope in silence. They were all growing tired, and were mostly immersed in their own thoughts. Even Custard was quiet as he followed his mistress, and his tail, normally on the move the whole time, tended to droop a little limply.

They came to a fork in the road and, after a brief discussion, decided to take the right-hand path, as it appeared to be the more frequented of the two. Soon afterwards, Candice startled the others by breaking the profound silence that had accompanied their progress.

'Listen!'

'Now what is it?' Adam asked petulantly.

'Quiet!' she said. 'And listen!'

After about ten seconds' silence, Adam, a bit peevish at being spoken to so harshly, said, 'I can hear it now. But I've no idea what it is.'

'I have,' said Belle. 'It's water.'

'Water?' he questioned.

'She's right,' agreed Candice. 'You've got good hearing, Belle, nearly as good as mine.'

The younger girl blushed with pleasure and Adam,

still more peeved because he hadn't come in for any praise, said, 'But what can it be – an underground river?'

'Probably. Perhaps some kind of waterfall as well. Let's go and see.'

The thought that something different lay ahead spurred them on and they hurried along the tunnel, negotiating bends and curves and corners as the tunnel twisted and turned, while all the time the noise grew louder.

Five minutes later the tunnel ended abruptly, on the brink of a deep chasm. The three adventurers stood on the edge, lanterns raised, and they peered down. But the green light was now weak and they could only catch a glimpse of the rushing torrent that foamed along the bottom of the chasm, which must have been thirty or more metres deep.

Across the other side, dimly visible, was a shiny rock-face, and a tunnel mouth much like the one in which they now stood. And between the two orifices was suspended a flimsy bridge, consisting of one thick interwoven rope for the feet, and two thinner ropes running parallel to and above the first one, presumably for hand-holds. Adam and Belle viewed the fragile contrivance with considerable dismay.

'Do you mean to say we've got to cross THAT?' quavered Belle.

'If you wish to get to the other side – yes,' replied Candice in a matter-of-fact voice.

'There's no other way, Belle,' said Adam. 'We can't go back now. And it doesn't look TOO bad,' he added, with half-hearted reassurance.

They stood staring at the frail structure, until Candice

said, 'Well, it won't get any better just looking at it. Who's going first?'

'What about Custard?' asked Belle, glancing at the furry head peering out of the blonde girl's shoulder-bag.

'No, he's too young to go first,' said Candice, tongue in cheek.

'Oh, YOU know what I mean!' said Belle.

'Yes I do. And don't worry about him. I climbed up that rope with him in my bag, so crossing a bridge should be child's play.'

'Well, if you have a child handy, send him across first,' said Adam with a clumsy attempt at humour.

'Well, for THAT you can go first,' said Candice maliciously. Then, in a more natural manner, 'And I'll bring up the rear.'

Adam hooked his lantern onto his belt and set one foot gingerly onto the lower rope. He held tightly to the upper ropes and moved his other foot past the first one. Cautiously he ventured out onto the slender bridge, gripping the hand-ropes as hard as he could, trying not to look down into the dark depths that were tumultuous with the rush, gush and gurgle of the underground river far below.

'How does it feel?' Belle called out. Adam paused to consider. 'Alright,' he said eventually. 'Flimsy – but I think it'll bear our weight.'

'Perhaps I ought to hang on until he's across?' Belle asked Candice.

'No,' replied Candice, after giving it some thought. 'It looks strong enough to bear a dozen people, and we'll only waste time going over one by one. Besides, there are only two lanterns and one of us would have to cross without one, which wouldn't be very pleasant. Off you go.'

Belle set her feet and hands onto the ropes, steeled herself to the task, and edged slowly along after Adam. Candice made sure Custard was securely tucked into her bag, then she followed Belle. Slowly but surely the three of them moved out across the black chasm above the rushing waters, the ropes swaying freely but otherwise feeling strong and firm.

At one moment there was an unusual commotion in the waters below – they heard a ghastly snapping and gurgling sound, accompanied by a splashing swishing disturbance of the water's surface. Belle could not help but look down, and the sight of the deep black ravine and the glimmer of white foam as the river dashed itself against the many rocks in its path was an unnerving one. She gasped, shut her eyes tightly and halted, clinging onto the ropes grimly as she hung, swaying in mid-air. Candice edged up to her, released one hand and put her arm round Belle's quivering body, speaking to her with gentle reassurance.

'I ... I looked down,' said Belle unsteadily. 'I know I ... I shouldn't have ... but I c-couldn't help it. I'll be alright in a m-moment.'

'What's happening?' Adam called from his position in front. He was now halfway across and feeling more and more confident.

'Carry on!' Candice shouted to him. She had to shout to make herself heard above the roar and tumult of the torrent in the confined space of the ravine.

Adam restarted and the others followed. They were about two-thirds across when, without any warning, the black mouth of the tunnel they were approaching was no longer empty. In the faint green light from his lantern Adam saw a hideous figure appear. It was very bulky and seemed to be covered in a slimy green leathery hide. It had thick, sturdy legs and a prehensile tail. Much of the head was covered in a mass of wavy, snake-like growths, but Adam also caught a glimpse of huge, glowing red eyes and a gaping crimson maw. He gave a gasp of horror and stopped dead. The two girls also halted, craned their necks to see what was happening and spotted the horrific apparition. Belle screamed and – as if in answer – the creature slashed at the ropes attached to the rock-face with great armoured claws. The fragile bridge swayed violently. Candice gave a shriek, one rope snapped, another followed and the next second the three adventurers fell down, down, down and down again into the dark abyss, hitting the water with three great splashes and sinking deep under the surface of the swift-flowing river.

5

Adam remembered little of what happened next. He had no real idea of the passing of time, or of events. His sudden descent from the rope-bridge, and his equally sudden immersion in water that was icy cold, extremely wet and fast-flowing, was followed by a maelstrom of disconnected impressions. The river's icy shroud bore him along with irresistible force on a chaotic nightmare journey full of ups and downs, twists and turns, dashes and eddies, splutters, splashes, gurgles and gasps. He was tossed by the water hither, thither and yon, shoved, drenched, pummelled, carried along, whirled about, thrown up and dragged down, until he didn't know which way was up. And then he became dimly aware of something tightening round his neck, and of being pulled backwards, then upwards, and of arms supporting him, and strange voices, and dim faces appearing out of, and disappearing into, gloom. He was aware of being undressed, and wrapped in blankets, and lying on something soft, cocooned in dry, secure warmth, and a thick liquid that tasted like the most delicious stew in all the world being spooned into his mouth. Gradually the shock and terror and fright dissolved like snow under the summer sun, and he slept.

He was woken up by a tongue rasping over his fingers. The next moment a cold, wet nose was pushed into the palm of his hand. He opened his eyes to behold Custard's liquid brown gaze resting on his face. He reached out and fondled the small, wriggling body.

'Custard, old fellow,' he murmured. 'What are you doing here?'

Custard yelped excitedly and leapt upon him, trying hard to lick his face. He pushed the dog away and in doing so happened to look sideways. He saw Candice about a metre away, sitting up, her brown shoulders bare as she held a blanket about her torso. She gave him a brilliant smile.

'So you're back with us at last,' she remarked.

He gazed at her and suddenly remembered all that had happened. He sat up, realised he had no clothes on and drew his blanket up to his waist.

'Where are we?' he asked, trying to appear unconcerned at his lack of attire. After all, he reasoned to himself, it looked very much as though Candice was similarly unclothed.

'At a rough guess, in a cave, somewhere inside the Mountain.'

'Where's Belle?'

'The other side of you. She's still fast asleep.'

He turned his head and saw that Belle lay on a palliasse similar to his own, covered up to her shoulders by a blanket. Her eyes were shut, her face composed and she breathed evenly. He felt a sudden surge of an emotion new to him (not affection, surely?) and to disperse it he looked around. They were in a commodious low-roofed cavern lit by lamps hanging from small brackets fastened to the walls. These lamps were not green and flickering like the glow-moth lanterns, but instead gave off a cheerful orange light. The three palliasses they lay on were grouped together in the centre of the cavern. On a large wooden box nearby stood a saucepan and three brown mugs and – wonder of wonders! – their three shoulder-bags, looking wrinkled but reasonably dry. There were strange ornaments on the rock-walls, made of some material akin to earthenware but in a dark green colour; it was impossible to see what they represented. The uneven floor was covered by rugs woven from thick thread in plain colours. In one corner there was an archway, with darkness beyond.

'So ... we all survived, including Custard,' he said wonderingly, recalling the terror evoked by the sudden plunge into the icy black waters of the underground river.

'Looks like it,' agreed Candice cheerfully. 'Assuming of course that Belle is alright and hasn't broken anything.'

'I am ... and I haven't ... I don't think.'

This was Belle's voice and they turned to see her peering at them from under her blanket. Hearing her voice, Custard raced round to her and performed his usual canine song-and-dance act of welcome.

'Where are we?' she asked sleepily, reaching out to fondle the dog.

'In a cave, inside the Mountain,' replied Adam. 'Do you remember falling in the river?' She nodded. 'Well, someone must have rescued us.'

'Us ... and Custard ... and our shoulder-bags,' added Candice. 'But I think we lost the lanterns.' She pondered. 'Now I come to think of it, I can remember being pulled out of the water, and someone undressing me and wrapping me in this tickly blanket, and giving me hot soup, and telling me to go to sleep. Can either of you?'

They both agreed that they had had a similar experience. Belle peered under her blanket. 'Oh goodness!' she said. 'I REALLY am ... er ... undressed.' Her face was pink.

'I only hope that whoever took our clothes is drying them for us to put on again,' said Candice wryly. 'If not, we shall look pretty silly walking around in these blankets – apart from being tickled to death by them.'

'A bird in the hand is worth two in the bush,' remarked Belle, still pink with embarrassment.

'I wonder who it was?' puzzled Adam. 'I seem to recall little people with furry hands fussing round me. I suppose it couldn't have been those troglodytes we met earlier?'

'No,' replied Candice positively. 'I told you they couldn't stand light, so they wouldn't have all these lamps around.'

'Then who? And, come to think about it, why are most of the creatures down here so small?'

'I should have thought that was obvious,' said Candice tartly. 'Think of all these narrow passages and small chambers and low roofs down here: it's evolution at work. What with the constricted space, and the lack of sunlight and fresh air, no wonder they all look puny and feeble and sickly.'

'Who WAS this wise man who taught you so much, Candice?' Belle asked enviously. 'I'd really like to meet him.'

'He died,' Candice replied briefly.

Adam hurriedly changed the subject and said, 'That horrible monster that cut down the bridge wasn't puny or feeble or sickly. So what do you make of him? Why

95

did he have to be like that? We hadn't done him any harm. Why did he act so mean?'

His tone was injured, as though he regarded it as a personal affront.

'How he look, pliss?'

The words came in a strange inhuman voice, thin and reedy, from the direction of the archway. They turned and saw a small creature standing just inside the chamber, looking at them with comical gravity. He had a round, furry face with eyes like large, brown buttons, large furry ears, a small brown nose and furry cheeks. His small, stocky figure was clad in a green waistcoat over a red shirt tucked into chocolate-brown trousers. His shoulders were slightly hunched, and his hands were like paws, with four digits on each instead of five.

He trotted forward and repeated his earlier question. 'How he look, pliss?'

'How who look?' queried Adam, groping for understanding.

'Creature who cut ropes,' said the little furry creature.

'Oh!' Adam described what he had seen and the dwarf nodded and said in his squeaky voice, 'Him not good. Not good at all. Member of sub-order *Lacertilia* – iguanas, lizards, geckos. Not good. They not like anybody. You keep away, pliss?'

'We'll do that alright,' said Adam. 'And who might you be?'

'Not might be. Am. Me Uno, number one servant. Me and other servants pull you from river, remove clothes, give soup. You sleep. Better now?'

'Where are our clothes?' Belle asked with some anxiety.

'Soon be dry. You want eat, drink, pliss?'

Being thus reminded of the fact that inside them there was a deep and aching void, and Belle being (partially) relieved about her clothes, they all nodded energetically. The dwarf went away and returned with a loaded tray, followed by two other dwarfs also bearing trays. Their short legs made them look as though they were trotting all the time. Adam, observing that the newcomers wore long, voluminous dresses, and had their heads covered in funny hats like sou'westers, assumed that they were female.

'Other servants,' announced Uno. 'Duo and Treo. Duo cook, Treo clean.' The trays were placed in front of the three invalids, the girls somehow managing to secure their blankets up in their armpits to maintain some degree of modesty. Adam tucked his blanket round his waist and tried to appear at ease. The two female dwarfs trotted out, giggling.

'And what do you do, Uno?' asked Candice as she ate. The food was a kind of thick stew and it smelled and tasted so good that no one felt inclined to mar the proceedings by enquiring as to the main ingredient.

'I look after master, pliss.'

'And who is that?'

'My master Castroglio, pliss.'

All three started violently.

'You mean ... this is Castroglio's abode?' gasped Adam. 'He ... he REALLY lives here?'

The dwarf bobbed his furry head.

'Well, I'll go to the foot of our stairs!' said Adam reverently. 'Hear that, you two? Would you believe it? We've been and gone and done what we set out to do – we've found Castroglio.'

'We?' said Candice with pardonable displeasure.

'Yes, sorry, Candice,' said Adam at once. 'You got us here. It was you who guided us to the great man himself. And Belle had better believe he exists, eh Belle?'

Belle was defiant. 'I'll believe in him when I see him,' she said.

'You see him soon,' said Uno. 'Eat, drink, put on clothes, I take you see him.'

'That's great!' gasped Adam and he began to eat very quickly, cramming his mouth full of the delicious stew. When he spoke again, his voice was muffled. 'Well, you go and fetch our clothes like a good lad. And you two girls, you get a move on. You've hardly touched your food. We don't want to waste any time, do we?'

'I don't see why we have to hurry,' objected Belle. 'We spent a lot of time getting here: a few more minutes won't make any difference.'

'Oh yes it will,' contradicted Adam obstinately.

'Well, I'm not going to bolt my food just for you. The trouble with you is that you're selfish. You think of no one but yourself the whole time.'

'I am NOT selfish!'

'You ARE selfish.'

'I'm not.'

'You are.'

'I'm not.'

'You are.'

'Not.'

'Are.'

'Not.'

'Are.'

'For pity's sake put a sock in it,' ejaculated Candice.

98

'If you'd only stop arguing for a minute, you might have enough breath left for eating.'

Recognising the truth of this, Belle and Adam grinned sheepishly and applied themselves to the contents of their trays.

Ten minutes later, having finished the meal and arrayed themselves in their dry clothes (which had been cleaned and pressed and brought to them by the two furry little females), they were taken by Uno through the archway, along a series of corridors and up and down several flights of steps hewn out of the solid rock. The way was lit at intervals by small lamps hanging from metal hooks projecting from the walls, which provided the same cheerful orange light that they had found in their chamber. The last flight of steps – upwards – ended at a stout wooden door, at the side of which a lamp suspended from an ornate iron bracket illuminated a wooden board inscribed 'OFFICE – PLEASE RING'.

There was a small brass bell hanging from a hook, with a neat little padded hammer nearby. Uno took the hammer and struck the bell. It responded with a surprisingly deep tone. A voice from within the room said 'Enter'. Adam experienced a thrill of excitement: at last he was to meet the fabled sorcerer about whom he had heard so many legends. The dwarf opened the door, which replied with a long drawn-out creak of protest.

'Visitors, master,' announced Uno in a deeply respectful voice. He looked at the three adventurers. 'You go in, pliss.'

Candice held Custard securely in her arms and led the way into the room. The door closed behind them.

6

The chamber in which they found themselves was large, octagonal in shape and high-ceilinged, whilst all the walls, save the one in which the door was located, were lined with shelves overflowing with old books of every size, thickness and colour. The only light came from an oil lamp standing on a large black desk, so that most of the room was in shadowy darkness. The top of the desk was littered with a wide variety of objects, mostly ancient tomes, sheaves of paper and scrolls tied with ribbons. There was also a white skull, a dark brown carved box that looked incredibly old, an abacus, a strange device consisting of a brass circle revolving inside a larger brass circle, a big ink-pot with a quill-pen sticking out of it, a crystal ball, a conical hat ornamented with stars and crescent moons, and – most unusual of all – a cage containing a big black bird that stared at them with unwinking beady eyes. It was so motionless that it might have been stuffed.

Behind the desk, in a high-backed armchair, sat a man. He was clearly quite old, with a lined, leathery face and a profusion of whiskers. Large spectacles with thick lenses hid his eyes, which were overshadowed by bushy eyebrows and flanked by cadaverous cheeks. He was hunched in the chair and wore a voluminous black robe, from the sleeves of which protruded wrinkled claw-like hands on thin wrists. He was gazing down at a book which lay open in front of him, and did not raise his eyes as they clustered in a sheepish group in front of his desk. When he failed to acknowledge their presence, Candice walked boldly forward.

'How do you do, Mr Castroglio,' she said firmly. 'We're the ones your servants rescued from the underground river. We'd like to thank you and them for looking after us.'

The old man raised his eyes and stared at her, then at the others. He gave a violent start and his ancient hands began to feel and fumble about the desktop, his deep-sunken eyes behind the thick spectacles darting all over the place.

'Where's my hat?' he asked in a feeble querulous voice. 'Where's my sorcerer's hat? I'm a sorcerer, you know. I've GOT to wear my sorcerer's hat for visitors. No other hat will possibly do. Where is it?'

Candice picked up the conical headgear and handed it to him. He took it with trembling fingers and, with an effort, lifted it onto his head.

'That's better. That's SO much better. Now I can meet you properly.' He leaned forward and peered at them myopically through his lenses. 'Er ... who did you say you were?'

'We're the ones that got rescued from the river,' explained Candice patiently. 'We wish to thank you.'

'Don't thank me,' said the old man peevishly. 'Must've been my servants. They're very good at rescuing people, you know. Strange ... that's his name – Uno. And the other two ... er ... what's-her-name and er ... thingamy-jig. Very good at rescuing people, they are. Do it all the time. You must meet 'em some time. Well worth the effort.'

'We HAVE met them,' said Candice, still patient. 'They were the ones who rescued us. And they've looked after us splendidly. They've been very kind.'

'Hey? What kind did you say?' the old man asked.

'No, I said your servants have been very KIND to us,' said Candice, making great efforts to maintain her calm.

'Hey? Who've been very kind to you?'

'Your servants – Uno and the other two, Duo and Treo,' replied Candice, wondering how much longer she could keep her cool.

'Oh … er … them! They're good workers, all four of 'em – or is it five? Never can remember. But they're very good. You ought to meet 'em, you know. Yes, and him as well. He's my number-one servant – or is it number two? He's a good fellow.'

Candice turned and looked hopelessly at her two comrades. In the meantime, Castroglio picked up his crystal ball and peered into it, his eyes blinking down at the glowing orb, his large spectacles sliding down his long nose. His three visitors exchanged glances of despair. Adam felt particularly bitter. He thought, 'So THIS is the legendary sorcerer and wizard I've travelled so far to see – this fumbling, bumbling senile and decrepit old dodderer! What hope have I of obtaining any sort of protection – or, indeed, help of any kind – so that I can carry on with my hazardous quest?' Belle was thinking, 'What chance have I of learning any more about the present whereabouts of my brother from this poor old man who should be in a home?' And Candice, having quite lost her patience, was thinking, 'Why did I waste my time bringing these kids here? This ancient half-witted foozling old ninny is clearly of no use to anybody at all.'

The old man suddenly let out a loud cackle, startling them and interrupting Adam's rather doleful train of thought. He was now peering at them from under his bushy eyebrows.

'Fumbling, bumbling, senile and decrepit old dodderer, am I? Poor old man who should be in a home, am I? Ancient half-witted foozling old ninny, am I?' As each of them stood amazed that he had divined exactly what they had been thinking, even using the same words, he went on, in a voice that was suddenly strong and incisive. 'I'll thank all three of you to be a little more respectful to your elders and betters.' He shot a glance at Belle. 'You're very fond of repeating useful little adages, aren't you? Don't argue – I KNOW! Well, here's one for you. Never judge a book by its cover. Hey?'

'I ... er ... yes, I ... I agree,' stammered Belle.

'How do you know she likes adages?' gasped Adam.

The old man directed a keen glance at him.

'How do I know your name is Adam and that your two colleagues are named Belle and Candice?'

'That's easy,' replied Candice confidently. 'One of us must have talked in his or her sleep.'

The old man cackled again.

'Good try, girl, but not so. I know quite a lot about you. How, you may ask? Well, no, you may NOT ask. But I'll tell you. This crystal ball is not just an ornament, you know. It's a complicated and complex piece of equipment. VERY few people have learned how to use it. I am one. I am able to see things others cannot. For instance, I know that Adam has come a long way to ask me for help in his quest to find the Sacred Chalice of Saint Anthony. I know that he is an orphan and was brought up by the couple Rowland and that he has a dog named Biscuit.'

'He STILL could have said those things in his sleep,' said Candice doggedly.

The old man's blue eyes turned in her direction and she felt uneasy.

'I know that you are Candice of the Forest, that you live in the cave formerly occupied by the family of Boris the bear, and that your dog's name is Custard. And, in case you think that you said all that in your sleep,' he added maliciously, 'you may like to know that I knew your father before he died. He was a good and wise man.'

'That's the answer!' crowed Candice. 'You learned all about me from him, and recognised me.'

'Talk sense, girl. How could he have told me about your residing in Boris's cave, which happened after he died?' asked the old man with unassailable logic. 'But that is not all. I know that Belle has left an ailing father, a hard-working mother and a young sister to come looking for her brother, who entered the forest two months ago and has not returned home.' He looked sharply at Candice as she opened her mouth to speak. 'There is no need to say anything. I know many things. That is because I AM a sorcerer, despite how I may appear to you. How else do you think my servants were able to rescue you from the river? I sent them to the landing-stage, just as you swept past, helpless in the grip of the torrent.' He paused. 'You came to me for assistance yet, seeing my appearance and accepting my foolery at face value, you decided that I was useless and unable to help you in any way.

Perhaps this will teach you not to rely on first impressions.'

'Very well,' said Candice angrily. 'We've learned our lesson. Now let us depart: we'll do without your help.'

'No we won't!' cried Belle indignantly. 'Speak for yourself, Candice. We were wrong and I for one am certain he CAN help us. Don't you think so, Adam?'

'Well ... I don't know...' said Adam hesitantly.

The old man cackled once more.

'It is as I thought. The one who wants help most believes in me. The one who needs no help wants none.' He rose to his feet and, to the surprise of the onlookers, he was very tall, well over two metres in height, and very gaunt, so that he towered over them. His decrepitude and senility dropped from him like a discarded cloak and he radiated force, wisdom and a benevolent arrogance.

'Now, hear me! I give help to those who need it. Candice has no need of it and therefore I have nothing to say to her. You, Adam, came to me in the hope that I could supply you with an amulet to protect you from the evils that face anyone foolish enough to attempt to steal the Sacred Chalice of Saint Anthony. Yes, I said "steal". Because the Chalice does not, and cannot, belong to you. Nor did it ever belong to the Lord of Moldavia. It does not even belong to its present owner. It is, in fact, the property of the High Priests of Zaire, and it has been so since the beginning of time.'

He resumed his seat and looked at them, holding them in thrall with his hypnotic gaze.

'Let me tell you about it. Long long ago, when the world was much younger than it is now, an upright and truly religious man called Anthony preached the doctrines of goodness and truth in a land where evil and lies held sway. He was accused, by wicked men jealous of his fame and popularity, of blasphemy and the black arts. He was arrested and brought before the cruel ruler of the land, who ordered him to undergo trial by poison. A chalice was prepared, containing a mixture of hemlock, belladonna, aconite and henbane – all deadly poisons. If he drank it and died, he was guilty. If he drank it and survived, he was innocent.

'He took the cup and fearlessly drained it: and he did not die. The people took it as a miracle, as an intervention by the Great Ruler in the Sky; Anthony was canonised, and the Chalice became a holy relic. It was given to the High Priests of Zaire to cherish and protect, a task they have carried out for centuries.

'Then, many years ago, the Abbey of Zaire was pillaged, and the Chalice stolen. It vanished from all knowledge. Years later it appeared in the possession of the Lord Polmeny of Moldavia, and was kept in his museum, watched over day and night by a special corps of guards, under a sector captain named Arrowsmith.

'More recently – some three years ago – the museum was attacked by a large raiding party. They were heavily armed and broke into the palace and slaughtered all the museum guards with the exception of the sector captain, who was left bound and gagged. Only the Chalice was stolen. After the event, the sector captain was accused of being an accomplice of the raiders. There was no evidence and he was never put on trial, but the disgrace was too much for him and he died soon afterwards.

'The Chalice disappeared again. Rumours have circulated ever since that it lies somewhere underground, behind a gate, and that the gate is protected by an unknown Guardian said to be both terrible and invincible.'

A look of complacency suffused his wrinkled countenance. 'Yet I, the Great Castroglio, have been able to ascertain the whereabouts of the Chalice. I ... and I alone ... know where it is hidden.' The look of complacency was replaced by a frown. 'But I have not yet been able to discover who or what is the Guardian. There is a barrier, created by a sorcerer who, although I dislike intensely to admit it, is very nearly my equal in calibre and skill.'

He turned his daunting gaze to Adam.

'Having heard all that, is it your intention still to steal the Chalice?'

Adam straightened his shoulders. 'Yes,' he said defiantly.

'Adam!' cried Belle, deeply distressed. 'How could you?'

Castroglio stared at him, clearly puzzled.

'I do not understand,' he said at last. 'You are not a bad boy, yet you intend...' He sat down heavily, thought for a moment, then gazed into the crystal ball.

'Don't worry about me, Mr Castroglio,' said Adam hastily. 'Belle needs your help more than I do.'

The sorcerer ignored him, polished up the crystal ball with a black cloth, then stared into it again.

'Look, we can't hang around here,' Adam said hurriedly to the others. 'He's not going to help any of us. Let's go and...'

'What's the sudden rush?' asked Candice with surprise. 'I think he can help Belle. Why are you so keen to leave all of a sudden?'

'You and Belle can stay,' said Adam, moving agitatedly

towards the door. 'I've got to leave now. I've got better things to do with my...'

'Stay!' thundered Castroglio. 'Adam, I can help you as well.'

'No you can't. And in any case I don't WANT any help from you. I can manage on my own without...'

'Don't contradict me,' said the sorcerer in a deep voice. Then his tones softened. 'I know now why you are so agitated, my boy. It is nothing to be ashamed of. Your motives, although misguided, are wholly praiseworthy. Your name now is Rowland, but only by adoption. What was your name before?'

Adam remained silent and the sorcerer went on. 'No need to answer. It was Arrowsmith – right?'

'Arrowsmith?' ejaculated Candice. 'You mentioned that name just now.'

Belle said, 'The sector captain at the Museum who...' Then she stopped.

Castroglio nodded, his eyes on Adam. 'He was your father, was he not?'

Adam bowed his head and nodded.

'And you came to ... to remove the Chalice from its present location, NOT to steal it, but to return it to the person you thought to be the rightful owner, and thus restore your father's good name.'

Adam nodded again.

'Oh Adam, how marvellous!' breathed Belle, clutching his hand.

'I know my father is – was – innocent,' said Adam doggedly. 'This was the only way I could think of to do anything about it. You see,' he added sadly, 'there's no proof of his innocence – none at all.'

Castroglio bent his head again and focused once

more on the crystal ball. The study was silent save for small rustling noises from the black bird in the cage, which was now moving restlessly on its perch, although still keeping its beady eyes on them.

Finally Castroglio raised his head again.

'I cannot be sure if he was innocent or not,' he said. 'There is still that barrier... But I can tell you where you may be able to find the answer. But let me deal with Belle first.' His deep-set eyes turned in her direction. 'You I can help. Your brother Damon passed this way some eight weeks ago. He came along the river in a boat. He was on a pilgrimage to view the Chalice and had, I am certain, only the best of intentions. I told him where he might find the Chalice and I will give you, Belle, the same information which will be of interest to Adam also.'

He leaned back in his chair and pressed the tips of his fingers together in a scholarly manner.

'The Chalice lies in a dungeon beneath the Castle Grimaldi, which is to be found on the Island of Jade in the Sea of Azure. The Lord of the castle, and the illegal possessor of the Chalice, is the Black Baron of Xakkara – a clever sorcerer and a very evil man. Beware of him: I believe he is the creator of the barrier that prevents me from finding out about the dreaded Guardian. It was he who planned and directed the attack on the Moldavian Museum, and he will know about your father, Adam. But it will be of no earthly use appealing to him: he will only laugh in your face and throw you to his Guardian. And it will do you no good to steal the Chalice.'

Once more the sorcerer concentrated his gaze into the crystal ball. To Adam's surprise, sweat stood out in beads on the wrinkled brow and a pulse beat fast in the temple. Finally he looked up, and wiped the sweat from his forehead with a cloth.

'Once more I have been unable to break through the barrier completely. But I believe that there is one man in the castle who may be able to help you. He is known as the Lord of the Treasury. If you are able to reach him, you may know more. Whether it will be good news or bad, I cannot say.'

He waved aside profuse thanks from both Belle and Adam and continued to speak. 'And now, you would like to know how to get to the Island. The underground river that runs through the Mountain flows out to the Sea of Azure at the Gulf of Flamingoes. You must go that way, and sail across the Sea, heading north-west, until you reach the Island. It is a journey of at least two days.'

His wrinkled face broke into a smile as he saw the looks of dismay and despondency that appeared on the faces of his audience.

'Do not despair! I have said that I will help you. I have a small vessel that I propose to place at your disposal. But it requires skilful handling and I know that you do not possess this skill. I will therefore ask Uno to accompany you. He has much experience in sailing and he has, I know, conceived a liking for all three of you.'

'A friend in need is a friend indeed,' said Belle with gratitude.

Castroglio smiled briefly at her, then turned to Candice. 'I assume you will be going too?'

'Think I'd better,' she nodded. 'After all, we've come this far together. I reckon I have to finish the job.

Besides, someone's got to keep these fractious children in order.'

Before Belle or Adam could protest, Castroglio continued. 'Very well. Remember, on board the vessel Uno will be the captain and you must obey him. On land he will be your guide and servant. Now you must go. I will instruct Uno in his duties and he will collect you from your chamber. Be ready to leave in thirty minutes.'

Once again he brushed aside their thanks and the next moment Uno had appeared and ushered them outside, where one of the female dwarfs met them and conducted them back to their cave. They spent the next half-hour in excited discussion about their talk with the sorcerer and the next stage of their journey, and in preparing their shoulder-bags.

Finally Uno appeared. He had added to his attire by donning a peaked cap which he wore at a rakish angle on his furry head and which gave him a jaunty nautical air. He also wore a short sword dangling from his belt. He led them along passages and down steps until the party emerged onto a rock jetty lit by more orange lamps. The underground river gushed from a narrow ravine on their left, foamed past the jetty with many a rush, splutter and gurgle, and disappeared into another ravine. Secured to the jetty by a painter was a small, bright-blue sailing dinghy, rocking in the swell created by the river's speed. The boat had a furled yellow sail, and white lettering on the bow spelt out 'Kingfisher'.

'On board, pliss,' requested Uno.

As they stepped in, breathless with anticipation and excitement, they saw that the boat also contained rolled-up oilskins, a large hamper, tools and oars. Under Uno's direction, Adam and Candice sat at the oars, Uno took the tiller, and Belle untied the painter; Custard stood in the bows and yelped at the water rushing past. The boat swerved out into the current and was borne, rocking and swaying, along the river and into the dark maw of the ravine.

PART THREE

THE ISLAND

1

The Island rose up out of the deep blue ocean like a great green jewel (hence its name), iridescent in the bright sunlight, resplendent with beauty. It was, as islands go, on the large side, being very roughly circular in shape and measuring some thirty kilometres from north to south, and the same measurement from east to west. Apart from the strand of golden beach that encircled it like an amber necklace, it was clad in verdant emerald forest as dense as a bear's pelt. From the gently-sloping beaches it rose and fell in a series of irregular hills and valleys, and these led irresistibly upwards to a low mountain about one thousand metres in height and clothed in the same blanket of woodland almost to the summit. Only the last one hundred metres or so were without trees, and even then they were covered in thick grass, interspersed by clumps of purple heather, explosions of yellow gorse and sunbursts of golden broom.

Despite the sunshine, the hills and hollows of the Island were wreathed in a strange brooding grey-white mist that lay low over the treetops and drifted about the escarpments, extending long dismal fingers into the valleys.

The ocean surrounding the Island was calm and blue, but it had tides like all oceans, and these same tides ensured that rollers progressed with majestic regularity into the shore. They fell onto the sand with a shouting of waters, seething up to the warm beach to pluck at the edge of the vegetation before creeping back, tugging at the sand as they went, before being overwhelmed by the next wave.

Silent was the Island, a silent gem in a serene sea, almost as though it were waiting with baited breath for something momentous to happen, for someone to come along and disturb its serenity, to wake it from a long, exquisite sleep.

The boat named *Kingfisher* rocked in the swell as Adam, Belle, Candice, Uno and Custard stood together in the bows and stared towards the Island, watching it shimmer in the heatwaves rising up from the warm sea. Sunlight dazzled them, and they shaded their eyes as they looked.

'Island of Jade,' announced Uno, pointing with a self-important paw.

'It's bigger than I thought it would be,' commented Adam.

'And the journey didn't take as long as I thought it would,' added Candice. Her statement was followed by a bark from Custard, which seemed to signify his agreement with that assertion.

Belle didn't speak. She was conscious only of a faster-beating heart as she stared at the mysterious and beautiful Island wreathed in tenuous veils of mist, an unknown but fascinating enigma that seemed to float on the clear blue water. At last they had arrived at a place where, with luck, and perhaps with the approbation of the Great Ruler of the Skies (and possibly a bit of assistance from the same source) she might find her brother. Her excitement was tinged with apprehension and her hands trembled ever so slightly as she held onto the mast and shaded her eyes from the glare of the morning sun.

They were all silent, each preoccupied with his or her thoughts. Adam was thinking that Candice was right – the journey had not taken long. After their boat had left the jetty, the underground river had borne them on its foaming bosom through narrow ravines and wide tunnels, along shallow channels bestrewn with huge boulders requiring a deal of skilful navigation by Uno at the tiller. They had negotiated bends and curves, and experienced a brief but exhilarating stretch of rapids where both Uno's expertise and Adam's strength at fending off objects with his oar had seen them through.

There had been a strange journey across an underground lake, the water so deep that it had looked both black and sinister, the rock ceiling soaring above their heads into darkness like the high-vaulted and groined ceiling of a cathedral, so that when they spoke their voices echoed and re-echoed; when Custard barked it had seemed like blasphemy. Then followed more ravines and more tunnels, until finally the river had carried them out of the Mountain into broad daylight, and along between banks edged with luxuriant forest alive with brilliantly-hued birds and many small furry animals. It had taken them a while for their eyes to adjust to the daylight, and in the meantime the river had carried them along at a spanking pace, between ever-widening banks and with the depth of water increasing beneath their hull every metre.

Finally they had debouched into the Estuary of Flamingoes but unfortunately, for a reason they were unable to discover, they had not espied one single flamingo. The estuary widened and vanished into mist and then they were out on the Sea of Azure, the weather halcyon, the ocean calm. The weather had continued to favour them and the voyage to the Island had been interesting but uneventful. And now they stood off the Island itself, approaching it at a leisurely speed as the light breeze bellied the yellow sail.

Suddenly Belle broke the silence, giving a cry as she pointed.

'Oh look there! What's that?'

They swung round and saw a black, triangular fin cutting through the smooth water, heading towards them with deadly intent and at an alarmingly swift speed.

'Is it ... a ... a ...?' said Adam, going a bit pale.

'Shark,' replied Candice laconically.

'Oh Uno, can't we go any faster?' cried Belle with deep anxiety.

'Not possible,' replied Uno calmly. 'Cannot manufacture wind.'

Candice picked up a boat-hook from the bottom of the dinghy and stood with one foot up on the port bulwark, gripping her weapon in both hands.

'Get an oar each, you two,' she said to the others. 'Fend it off if you can. Nothing else we can do.'

The menacing fin approached the boat at a frightening rate until it was almost upon them. Adam caught a glimpse of a huge, sleek, dark-grey body sliding along just below the surface, and the next moment the bulbous nose struck the *Kingfisher*, making it shiver from stem

118

to stern and rock wildly. Candice maintained her stance without too much difficulty and jabbed at the shark as it glided under the hull, but missed. Belle lashed at it with her oar, without any effect. Adam lost his footing after a mighty but useless lunge and sat down in the bottom of the dinghy, gasping.

'Oh Adam, don't play about!' wailed Belle. 'It's attacking us again!'

'Who's playing about?' demanded Adam indignantly as he struggled to his feet and picked up his oar. 'I tripped over one of the thwarts. If a fellow can't...'

'Shuddering shrimps, here it comes again!' shouted Candice. 'All hands to repel boarders!'

The shark cleaved through the blue ocean like a streak of dark-grey oil and headed straight for the boat. CRASH! For the second time it struck the small craft head-on, and this time the impact was accompanied by the ominous sound of splintering timbers, whilst the *Kingfisher* shook and groaned under the violence of the onslaught. Again Candice jabbed, and this time she managed to puncture the shark's skin, though it appeared to have no visible deterrent effect. Adam also hit it with his oar, but had the frustrating feeling that this was quite useless, and probably only encouraged the huge brute in its deadly purpose.

'Miss Belle,' called Uno, as phlegmatic as ever. 'Kindly take tiller, pliss?'

Belle scrambled across and took Uno's place in the stern, whilst the furry dwarf – his peaked cap tilted even more rakishly than usual – ranged himself alongside Adam and Candice, a diminutive figure but stiff with resolution as he drew his short sword and prepared to enter the fray. Custard the dog had meanwhile decided that anything HE could do in the circumstances would be quite useless, and so he curled up in the bottom of the boat, by Belle's feet, staring up at her with pleading eyes. Despite her fears, she leaned down, stroked his fuzzy head and spoke to him reassuringly.

'Here it comes again!' shouted Candice, who seemed to have taken on the role of commentator and mistress of ceremonies. 'Take careful aim and try to kill it or wound it at least. If only we could...'

The shark attacked for the third time, like a sinister torpedo hurling straight at them. CRASH! There was more splintering of wood and the *Kingfisher* rocked madly, almost throwing the three poised at the side into the sea. This time it was Candice who lost her foothold and sprawled on her back with her brown legs waving in the air.

'Another one like that,' gritted Adam, 'and we'll ALL be over the side.'

Candice scrambled to her feet. 'We're not going to let THAT happen,' she cried with grim determination and gripped her boat-hook tightly. The shark slid beneath the hull and glided majestically away. The four occupants of the boat watched it anxiously (if not apprehensively), and saw the black fin make a 180-degree turn and head back in their direction.

'This could be the big one,' said Candice quietly, but with a slight tremor in her voice. 'Stand by!'

'Everyone calm, pliss,' said Uno unemotionally. 'Must kill this time.'

The long, grey shape ploughed towards them. As though the shark had by now decided that the dinghy and its occupants were suitable ingredients for a meal, it opened its huge jaws, revealing two rows of sharp white teeth, and its rate of approach increased. The dog whimpered, Belle screamed, the shark opened its jaws wider and Candice plunged the boat-hook deep into its cavernous month. It closed its jaws with a crunch, snapping the stout boat-hook like a matchstick. As it did so, Uno leaned over the side and stabbed deliberately and with unerring accuracy into its left eye. The next second the huge bulk struck the dinghy amidships. The small vessel reared up sideways and abruptly turned turtle, hurling its five occupants willy-nilly into the foaming sea.

For a short period of time all was confusion. Adam sank below the water, but at once realised what had happened and, fighting a sense of panic, paddled rapidly until he broke back to the surface. Shaking the moisture from his face, he looked round for the others, and immediately spotted Belle swimming about nearby. He was only a moderate swimmer, but had no difficulty in reaching her. As she saw him, there was a flurry by their side and Uno's head appeared about two metres away. He swam awkwardly towards them.

'You here – good,' he said. 'Where is Miss Candice, pliss?'

They dog-paddled and looked around anxiously.

'I've not seen her,' gasped Belle.

'Nor I,' panted Adam. 'But what about the shark?'

'Think he go – not like sword in eye,' replied Uno. 'But urgent find Miss Candice quickly, pliss.'

Adam prepared to dive below the surface to see if he could spot the blonde, but at that moment another head broke the surface, shaking water free from the eyes. It was Candice, her normally tanned face now pale.

'Custard!' she gasped. 'I can't find him!'

'Can he swim?' asked Belle, bobbing up and down beside Adam.

'Yes but ... I still can't find him.' Candice's voice was strained. 'He was in the stern with you, wasn't he, Belle?'

'Yes, but I haven't seen him since we turned over.'

'I suppose the shark couldn't have...' began Adam, but Candice halted him with a loud cry.

'Oh no, no, no!' she half-sobbed, and stared round desperately, as did the others. The sea stretched on all sides, calm and blue, innocent of ugly black fins or swimming dogs.

'At least the shark's gone,' said Belle with some relief.

'But where dog?' questioned Uno.

Candice upended herself and dived below the surface. Uno did the same. As they disappeared, Adam and Belle continued to look about them, hoping to spot the lithe animal. But they failed to do so, and a few minutes later Uno's drenched, furry head appeared. He swam towards them with short jerky movements and said, 'No sign dog. You see him, pliss?'

They shook their heads.

'Where's Candice?' asked Belle fearfully. 'Think she's alright?'

'Swim like fish,' Uno said placidly. 'She fine, except not find dog.'

'I'm going cold,' shivered Belle. 'I ought to swim to the Island. But ... supposing there are more sharks about?'

'No sharks,' Uno stated with confidence. 'Good – you swim to Island. Adam go too. I stay, take care Miss Candice. Pliss?'

Adam was reluctant to leave the spot, with Candice

122

still under the water and the dog still missing, but Belle pleaded with him to help her and so they set out for the shore, swimming slowly but steadily. It was not far and the sea was calm and of a reasonable temperature. The rollers helped them towards their goal and within ten minutes they felt the sand of the beach under their sandals. They plodded up through the breaking waves onto the warm, wet sand. When they reached the dry part of the beach, they collapsed and lay gasping for breath and dripping wet, enjoying the warmth of the sun on their tired bodies, and too spent to move.

2

After some five minutes Adam sat up on the sandy beach and stared out to sea. He let out a strangled gasp and rubbed his eyes disbelievingly.

'What's wrong?' asked Belle, feeling quite languid and reluctant to rise from her recumbent position or even open her eyes.

'The ... the boat!' articulated Adam. At this, Belle sat up very quickly, then echoed Adam's gasp. The *Kingfisher* was coming towards the shore under sail, riding the rollers with ease. Uno was at the tiller and Candice stood by the mast. Uno was still wearing his peaked cap! Adam and Belle scrambled to their feet and ran down to the water's edge. Within minutes the boat entered the shallows, the sail was furled and the hull grated on the sand. The two occupants leapt out and the four of them hauled the vessel further up the beach and secured it to a large and convenient rock.

'How on earth did you manage to right it?' asked Adam in amazement.

'Simple,' said Uno serenely, but with a touch of pride. 'Me know what to do. Miss Candice help. But we lost tools, food. So sorry pliss?'

'Not your fault, Uno,' said Belle at once. 'At least we still have our bags.' She turned to the blonde. 'But what about Custard?'

Candice looked very unhappy and her lips quivered.

124

'He … he…' she began, then suddenly let go of the boat as tears came into her eyes and rolled down her cheeks.

Adam felt helpless. He had had little experience of tearful girls and just did not know what to do. Uno likewise seemed at a loss to know how to proceed, but Belle put her arm round the unhappy girl's slender waist and hugged her.

'Cheer up, Candice dear,' she said. 'It's always darkest before the dawn, you know.'

She continued to talk to her soothingly and Adam, relieved that he hadn't got to do anything to help, turned to Uno. 'Drowned?' he asked, horrified.

'Not know,' replied the dwarf, shrugging his small shoulders. 'Not found. No reason dog dead. Maybe alive somewhere.'

'Hear that, Candice?' Adam said eagerly. 'Custard may still be alive. He can swim and he might easily have made it to the beach. Come on, be sensible: don't give up hope before you have to. I'll tell you what we'll do. We'll explore all the way along the beach as far as we can, both ways. Uno and Belle in one direction, you and me in the other. How's that?'

Candice dried her eyes and rapidly recovered her spirits.

'You're absolutely right, Adam.' She gave him a brilliant smile that made him blush and then said to the others, 'Sorry I acted so stupidly. Let's get going, shall we?'

Belle had an urge to query why Adam had chosen Candice as his partner in the search and not her. But just as she was about to speak she realised that not only would it expose the fact that she herself wanted to go with Adam (and nothing on earth would drag that admission from her at this stage) but also it would imply that she did not wish to go with Uno, and not for anything would she wish to hurt the furry little dwarf's feelings. So she kept silent and within minutes the four had separated, Adam and Candice going one way and Uno and Belle the other.

Adam and Candice plodded along the warm, golden sand, their eyes continually on the lookout for a small bedraggled black-and-white dog. They encountered frequent outcrops of jagged rock that they either had to skirt round or climb over. The sand was soft and it was far from easy going. Occasionally there were inlets where the ocean thrust slender fingers up shallow channels and they were forced to leap or wade across. They kept a wary eye open for the numerous crabs that were scuttling about the beach, observed the many starfish and jellyfish floating calmly in the rockpools and noted the thousands of shells of all shapes and sizes scattered here, there and everywhere. Meanwhile there were seabirds circling and planing above their heads, diving into the sea on their right, or perched on the rocks and eyeing the inmates of the pools with beady interest. On their left, the forest was alive with the noises and movements of innumerable but invisible specimens of wildlife at work and play. And the sun blazed down over the whole scene, helping to dry their wet clothes.

Candice was quiet and withdrawn. Adam, searching in his mind for something to say in order to break the silence, could not think of anything that would not have sounded trite or trivial. But eventually Candice came to a halt and looked at him with a stubborn expression and tight lips.

'There's no sense in going any further,' she said hopelessly. 'He couldn't possibly have swum THIS far. He was too small, his legs were too short, his little lungs...'

She stopped and a tear rolled down her cheek. Adam's tender heart was smitten by her obvious distress.

'You never know,' he said with more hope than confidence, 'the current might have carried him this far and he...'

He was interrupted by a tremendous flapping of wings emanating from the forest. They looked upwards and were stunned to see an enormous black creature fly up from the treetops. It was truly gigantic in appearance and shape, something like a cross between an eagle and a vulture, but its body was as big as a man's, whilst the huge black wings must have measured ten metres from wingtip to wingtip. Its talons were as big as human hands. The head was bald, the beak long, curved and predatory, the eyes gleaming like fiery coals. It reminded Adam of the Vulgel they had encountered inside the Mountain, except that this was four or five times as big and correspondingly more terrifying.

'Whistling weasels!' breathed Candice, suddenly very still. 'It's a Terra-Hawk – a larger version of the Vulgel. I had no idea they lived this far north. For goodness sake don't move: if it sees us we're done!'

Presumably because of its size, the Terra-Hawk was not a swift mover. Its great wings beat with slow deliberation as it ascended above the treetops and then cruised around, its bald head swivelling on its scrawny neck as it surveyed the terrain below with beady eyes. To their horror it sailed towards the ocean, coming in their direction, and before they could do anything about it the evil head had turned sideways and they knew that it had spotted them.

'Too late – it's seen us!' panted Candice.

As the giant bird banked, flapped its ponderous wings and then glided down towards them, Adam dragged his catapult from his bag, fitted a large pebble into the pouch and let fly. The pebble hit the bird on its underbelly and it gave a hoarse croak, but kept on coming. Candice picked up a large stone the size of an orange and, as the bird planed down towards Adam, she flung it with all her strength. It struck the bird on the side of its head and the startled beast gave a screech of pain and swerved sideways, flapping its ungainly wings even faster.

It flew slowly round in a half-circle, climbed into the upper air, then dived at them again, uttering hoarse cries of rage. Candice drew her knife and waited in a crouched position. Adam fired another pebble at the oncoming creature and hit it in the neck. It croaked again, but still came on. Adam turned to run; his foot slid into a patch of soft sand and he lost his balance, falling flat on his face. As the bird screeched in triumph and reached out for him with convulsively clawing talons, Candice slashed at its legs. The bird gave a ghastly squeal and again veered away, blood dripping from one dangling useless limb.

'Run!' gasped Candice. 'Make for the trees!'

Adam scrambled to his feet and together they raced up the beach towards the shelter of the forest. They were only too painfully aware that the fearsome predator was once again diving down towards them, but the soft sand hampered their progress and they were forced

128

to leap over stones and climb over rocks in their path.

Before they could reach the trees, Candice trod on a large stone cunningly concealed by a thin layer of sand, twisted her ankle and fell flat on her face, just as Adam had done. The next second, with a horrendous flapping of wings and a screech of evil pleasure, the bird was upon her. Adam was for the moment paralysed as he saw the great talons fasten into the bodice of Candice's animal-skin garment, but then he sprang to her defence. The bird had momentarily folded its wings as it settled on the prone girl and, almost without thinking, he grasped the edge of one of them and dragged on it with all his strength. The bird lost its balance and flapped its wings wildly, knocking Adam onto his back. But at the same time it released Candice, who immediately leapt up, seized the stone she had trodden on and hit the hawk with it. It squawked shrilly and rose clumsily in the air to escape the pain, and this respite enabled Adam and Candice to run the last few metres into the trees, where they crouched, gasping for breath. The hawk hovered for a while, croaking with frustrated fury, then veered off and flapped away down the beach.

'Thank goodness for that!' exclaimed Adam, panting. 'What an escape!'

They looked towards the Terra-Hawk to see whether it had decided to give up the unequal struggle and search elsewhere for food. It was about fifty metres away and, as they watched, it suddenly dived down and disappeared behind an outcrop of rock.

'It's found something else to eat,' commented Adam. 'We're safe now!'

'Oh look!' shrieked Candice. The Terra-Hawk rose up again, beating its wings in triumph and carrying in its talons a small black-and-white object that was wriggling and yelping frantically.

'Oh Adam!' breathed Candice, white-faced and clutching at his arm. 'It's Custard!'

The enormous bird flapped away from the beach towards the trees and passed over their heads. Adam saw that the blonde had been right: it WAS Custard struggling in the bird's claws, and presumably the predator was now heading for its lair to consume its prey in peace.

'It's going away!' moaned Candice. 'Oh, poor Custard! Adam, what can we do?'

The two gave frantic chase, racing between the trees into the forest. After about a hundred metres they arrived at a cleared space and saw the Terra-Hawk flapping round in slow circles. Adam picked up a stone, fitted it into his catapult and fired. This time his aim was deadly and the missile crashed into the bird's eyes. It gave a horrible scream, its talons opened convulsively, and the small white animal slipped from its grasp and dropped towards the ground, vanishing below the rim of what appeared to be a deep hollow in the centre of the clearing. A strange grey mist rose from the hollow and drifted about in ghostly veils. Adam fired a second stone and hit the bird in its side. It screeched, shook itself and flapped away and upwards, clearing the treetops and disappearing from sight.

'Oh good shooting, Adam!' exclaimed Candice, and he blushed with pleasure. Without waiting to see if the bird might return, Candice sped across the clearing towards the hollow and Adam followed as quickly as he could, without in any way being able to match her lightning pace. He arrived at the rim to find Candice staring down into the wreaths of mist, her earlier elation evaporating rapidly. The hollow was in fact a deep depression in the ground, at least fifty metres across. The grassy slopes descended steeply into a wide expanse of scummy green bog covering the bottom of the depression. Custard had dropped plumb into the middle and was, even as they gazed in petrified horror, sinking slowly into the thick, glutinous morass. Already its hindquarters and belly had been drawn under the repulsive green slime, and the little dog was now whining piteously as its short forelegs scrabbled helplessly at the revolting sludge.

'Oh my!' was all Adam could think of as he gazed with total helplessness at the pitiful sight.

'No ... Custard ... NO!' screamed Candice and without any warning she plunged headlong down the slope, took a tremendous running leap and soared out into the bog. Had she been taking part in an athletic contest she would have won the long jump on the spot – and possibly established a new world record. Her feet struck the morass about half a metre from the dog and as she sank into the slime she threw herself forward, clutched at the animal and with one superhuman effort dragged him upwards. He came free of the ooze with a loud squelch, and somehow she half-turned and flung the animal backwards. Adam rushed to the edge of the mire and managed to catch Custard just before he landed. He set the little dog down and Custard crawled a metre or two up the slope, collapsed with a weak shiver and lay panting, its body trembling and its small pink tongue lolling from its mouth.

'Oh Candice!' said Adam in blank despair. 'What now?'

She managed to twist herself round until she faced him, but all her struggles to escape from the all-enveloping quagmire were to no avail and, in fact, only succeeded in causing her to sink deeper. The bog was already up to her waist and creeping higher by degrees.

'I don't know,' she said. Her face was pale, but her voice was steady. 'What do you suggest?'

'I don't know, I don't know!' he cried, beside himself at his inability to think straight in such an emergency.

'You'll think of something,' she said. 'How's Custard?'

'Custard's alright,' he answered, wondering how she could possibly give attention to her pet at such a time. 'But what about you?'

'Try cutting down a long branch and dragging me out with it,' she suggested, her voice now hoarse with tension as she sank a little lower.

Adam raced up the slope to the forest, selected the longest sapling he could find, hacked at it until it came free and rushed back down to the morass. He almost sobbed with frustration when he discovered that the sapling was about two metres too short, and no amount of stretching arms on the part of both participants did any good.

'What can we do? What can we do?' he gasped, at his wits' end.

'Find a longer branch,' she said huskily. The slime was now covering her bosom so that she was having to hold her arms up over her head. Her hands were caked with mud.

'I couldn't see one,' he said in an agonised voice. He looked round desperately, then shouted 'HELP – OH PLEASE HELP!'

It was done in complete despair, but to his ineffable

joy a voice answered 'Coming!' and Uno and Belle appeared at the edge of the depression. They took in the critical situation at a glance. Belle ran down to join Adam, but could only stand beside him and shout encouragement to the girl in the centre of the bog. Uno had disappeared.

'Where did he go to?' Adam asked, relief turning to anger. 'UNO!'

The next moment the dwarf appeared and ran down the slope dragging behind him a huge log. He said to Adam, 'Throw to Miss Candice pliss.' Together he and Adam lifted the log and hurled it into the mire. It fell beside the blonde, and without hesitation she threw her upper half across it. By straining every muscle and sinew, and with the help of the log, which did not sink into the ooze, she was able to extricate herself sufficiently to pull the rest of herself out of the slime and onto the log.

'More logs,' said Uno. The three of them found another one, rolled it down the slope and hurled it to Candice. It landed nearer the edge and Candice was able to drag herself from one to the other. Another log was thrown, then another, until she had worked herself near enough to the dry land for them to assist her out. Immediately she collapsed and lay shuddering, her body covered from shoulders to feet in the green ooze, from which emanated a really frightful smell. She lay panting, whilst the others rested – well away from the source of the stench. Almost at once she tried to get up, gasping something about seeing how Custard was, but Belle reassured her that the dog was alright.

'However did you manage to land up in there?' she asked innocently. 'You should look before you leap, you know!'

Candice was too spent to answer, and Adam told the others what had happened. 'How did you manage to come along just in time?' he asked.

'We'd given up the search and were on our way back to meet you two,' explained Belle. 'We saw you disappear into the forest after that horrible big bird and thought you might need some help.'

'Thank goodness you did,' said Adam fervently.

'Amen to that,' added Candice, showing signs of a speedy recovery.

Uno looked down at her. 'You rest, pliss,' he said. 'We find water for drink and wash.' He wrinkled his small red nose. 'You smell bad, pliss?'

'I smell 'orrible,' agreed Candice, and suddenly began to laugh weakly. Her feeble efforts turned into wild hilarity, which proved so infectious that Adam and Belle joined in, until all three were rolling around on the ground, almost helpless with mirth.

Uno watched them, nodding approval but remaining serious.

'Good. Laughter release tension, express relief at survival. You carry on with much ha-ha, pliss?'

But his words and his sober demeanour only made them howl all the more.

3

They found a stream of clear, cool water meandering and tinkling between grassy banks, on its leisurely way towards the ocean. By this stream they rested and drank as much as they could, whilst Candice went a little further along downstream and behind some bushes, where she stripped, bathed and washed her simple garment. Belle and Adam gave Custard a good scrub in the water, which made him look as good as new, if not better, and afterwards he scampered like a mad thing up and down the grassy sward, stopping every now and then to shake himself violently, spraying whoever happened to be nearest with surplus moisture, thus eliciting cries of protest. It was near here, too, that they found some berries that Uno pronounced fit to eat, and they made a meal of them, enjoying the chance to rest and recuperate.

When Candice's garment was sufficiently dry for her to wear, they called Custard away from the copse in which he had spent the last ten minutes sniffing appreciatively at various unclassifiable but delicious smells, and they went on their way, with Uno in the lead and Adam bringing up the rear, heading inland away from the ocean and towards the mist-veiled hills and valleys of the interior.

On the way they discussed their encounter with the Terra-Hawk, and decided that (a) Custard had once again belied his old reputation and behaved with incredible heroism to swim ashore all by himself, and (b) it had been nothing more than a stroke of amazing good luck that the giant bird had picked the dog up within sight of the two searchers. The blonde girl once again praised Adam's marksmanship with the catapult, saying it was this as much as anything that had beaten off the Terra-Hawk, and Adam, whilst hurriedly denying it, blushed all over once more. (He decided that he had been blushing a bit too much lately and would have to curb it – his blood would soon get tired of surging up and down his body regardless).

On the way they cut suitable cudgels from the undergrowth so that they would have additional weapons in hand to supplement their existing armoury, which up to then had been fairly sparse.

A bit later on, Uno was leading along a track between tightly-packed trees when he came to an abrupt halt and held up a paw. His head, still sporting the peaked cap, was cocked to one side.

'Trouble?' called Adam from the rear.

'Have feeling not alone. Anyone else have same feeling?'

'Not yet,' replied Candice, keeping a tight grip on Custard's cord. 'What sort of feeling?'

'Fur behind neck prickle. Believe someone or something watching us.'

Everyone peered about them, being careful not to move.

'Blessed if I can see anyone, or anything,' confessed Adam.

'They take care not be seen,' replied Uno. 'Believe they want know who we are, what we want.'

136

'They?' questioned Candice. 'More than one?'

'Two, three, maybe more.'

'And what – or who – do you think they are?' Adam demanded, a bit impatient because he couldn't hear or see anything. 'Do you mean people like us, or...' He was going to add 'funny dwarfs like you' but decided not to.

Uno shrugged his small shoulders. 'Besides Castle occupants, species indigenous to Island lives here. Called Ornithomes – very little known. Believe Ornithomes likely. Everyone watch out.'

Uno set off once again and the column followed him, all present keeping a very wary eye open, especially in respect of the dense forest behind them, and all conscious of the same feeling mentioned by Uno – a prickling at the nape of the neck.

Presently the trees thinned out and they began to climb a grassy escarpment up into thin layers of white mist that eddied down from the steeper slopes above. Reaching the top of the escarpment, they came across a small lake. The four travellers, plus Custard, walked to the edge and stood looking at it. It was like a tarn suddenly encountered in the mountains: roughly circular, the margin fringed with spiky plants and masses of strange vegetation, the expanse of water silent, still and very dark, as though the wreaths of mists hovering over it prevented the sunlight from getting through. In the very centre of the lake was an islet, a small irregular hump of land not much more than twenty metres across, grassy but showing no other plant-life. Over the islet, the motionless lake and the surrounding mist-enshrouded hills hung a curtain of the deepest silence, invisible yet tangible.

'Look!' exclaimed Candice, pointing. 'There – on the little island.'

They saw that a wooden post was driven into the apex of the small outcrop of land, and bound to the post was a girl, clad in a long, white robe encircled at waist level by a golden belt. Her arms were fastened behind the post, her ankles bound, her mouth gagged. Her face was bowed, hidden by her long, fair hair. Adam blinked and refocused his eyes. He could not understand why he had not seen her at once.

'That's strange,' remarked Candice, echoing Adam's thoughts. 'I didn't see her at first. It's as though she suddenly appeared out of the blue.'

'Out of the mist more likely,' asserted Belle. 'It must have hidden her and drifted away when we approached.'

'I suppose so,' admitted Adam. 'She looks pretty solid to me.'

As though the girl on the islet had seen them, she lifted her face and began to struggle against her bonds, and they fancied they heard a low moan float across the intervening water to their ears.

'We've got to untie her!' exclaimed Belle. 'Uno, how do we get across?'

'Boat,' said the furry dwarf laconically, pointing along the lake-edge. A small dinghy was moored to a narrow post sticking up out of the water.

'I didn't notice that before, either...' began Candice, but Adam and Belle ignored her and ran along the fringe of the dark water until they reached the boat. Candice and Uno followed them, to find them embarked and impatient to be off.

'Shouldn't one of us stay behind?' suggested Candice.

'What for?' asked Adam.

And Belle said, 'I don't think we ought to split up.'

'I don't know why,' said Candice with some asperity. 'I just feel uneasy...'

'I'd feel more uneasy if we separated,' said Adam.

'United we stand, divided we fall,' Belle reminded them.

Adam looked at her fixedly, wondering just how many more proverbs she was going to come out with, but Uno said, 'Old saw very wise. All go together – more friendly, pliss?'

Candice shrugged and entered the dinghy, followed by Uno. Belle untied the painter then Uno and Adam took the oars and rowed across the still dark waters towards the islet. No one seemed inclined to speak and even Custard was subdued as he nestled in Candice's arms. As they approached the small hump of land, the bound figure at the stake writhed in helpless agony and they could hear whimpers and moans coming from behind the gag. The bows of the dinghy grated against the rock, Adam leapt out and secured the rope around a suitable outcrop, the others disembarked and in a bunch they ran up the slight slope towards the bound girl.

They had almost reached her when she and the post faded from their sight.

They stopped short, thunderstruck. She had vanished. One second she was there, the next second she had gone, completely and utterly.

'What the...!' ejaculated Adam incredulously.

'Oh my goodness!' gasped Belle.

'Jumping jackasses!' exclaimed Candice.

'Not good,' said Uno.

'I ... I wondered if it was a ... a hallucination,' stammered Adam. 'And ... and it w-was!'

They approached the spot cautiously. But there was no doubt about it. Adam bent down and examined the grassy mound.

'She never was here,' he reported. 'Look! There's no sign of a hole where the post would have been. There's nothing.'

'Not good,' repeated Uno. 'Necessary leave quickly pliss.'

They turned and ran rapidly towards the lake-edge.

'The boat!' cried Candice.

As they raced towards it, the boat behaved exactly as the girl had done and faded from view. They stopped at the water's edge and gazed in dumb amazement at the still surface of the lake. Not even a ripple was visible.

Uno found his voice first. 'Not good,' he repeated again. 'Powerful sorcerer somewhere here, big magic.'

'But why?' asked Belle, pale-faced again. 'Who's doing all this to us – and why?'

'Think means harm,' said Uno seriously. 'Trick to maroon us on island.'

'Well, that won't work!' said Adam derisively. 'Who needs a boat anyway? It's not far across. We can all swim that – even Custard!'

'Of course!' exclaimed Belle, cheering up.

'Not good,' said Uno for the fourth time. 'See?'

A couple of sinister flat shapes had appeared in the waters of the lake and now slid silently, like logs, towards them. They stared in horror at the scaly backs, the small pig-like eyes just above the surface, the undulating and immensely strong tails.

'Alligators!' said Candice.

'Or crocodiles,' added Belle helpfully.

140

'Well, swimming's out, that's for sure,' said Adam dejectedly. Then he brightened up. 'Hold on! How do we know they're real? Perhaps they're the same as the girl and the boat.'

'Yes, that's true,' agreed Belle.

'You might possibly be right,' acknowledged Candice begrudgingly. 'But now tell me how to find out. Who's going in to see?'

'Very difficult,' said Uno. 'Look real.'

They stood gazing at the floating reptiles with frustration.

'How are we going to tell whether they're alligators or crocodiles?' asked Adam.

'Does it matter?' asked Candice, staring at him.

'If we're going to be eaten, I'd rather like to know what by.'

'Oh, don't joke at a time like this!' wailed Belle. 'I don't want to be eaten, by alligators or crocodiles or anything else. I just want to get off this awful island and...'

She stopped speaking as the waters of the small lake about five metres from the edge began to boil and churn, as though it was being agitated violently from below. They watched in silent fascination. It was nothing to do with the log-like reptiles, who continued to float just under the surface, their beady eyes fixed on the marooned party. The agitation of the water increased and suddenly spatters of a thick red liquid appeared and they caught a glimpse of a great shoal of small fish fighting and tearing at one another with hideous ferocity under the water. Presently the frantic commotion quietened down and Candice said, in a husky voice, 'Piranha fish.'

141

Adam and Belle were speechless. They both knew about the small but incredibly evil little monsters that swam about in shoals and attacked or tore to shreds anything that was alive but wounded until only the bare bones remained. But Uno said, once more, 'Not good – if real.'

'I don't fancy testing the theory myself,' said Adam, trying to play it cool. Unfortunately he spoke with a voice that came out husky with tension.

'Whoever is doing all this, they're QUITE determined to keep us on this island,' said Belle tremulously.

'Yes, and I'm wondering why,' mused Candice. 'Is it that they don't want us to go any further – a sort of warning? Or...'

'Or what?' asked Belle.

'Or is something going to happen whilst we're here?'

'Like what?' demanded Adam.

At that moment they felt the islet move under their feet. It seemed to tremble and shake: vibrations penetrated through their soles and it felt as if it were no longer stationary. But they could not tell in which direction it was moving – if any.

'Like that,' said Candice, answering Adam's last query.

'What's happening?' gasped Belle, clutching at Adam's arm.

The answer came quite suddenly as water lapped around their sandals. They stared down in bewilderment. The water came in further and covered their feet. They retreated in disorder. The water followed.

'The lake is rising!' Adam cried.

'No – island sinking,' corrected Uno, straight-faced. 'Not good, pliss?'

Had they not been in such a parlous plight, his

serious face and tone would have caused them considerable hilarity. But laughter was the furthest thing from their minds. They backed away up the slope to the very centre, but the water followed, creeping up the slope after them and reducing the area of dry land to a small piece only about four metres across. Their fears were in no way alleviated by the continual boiling occurring in several places just under the surface of the water, denoting the presence of more piranha fish, whilst a number of flat, scaly shapes had joined the original few, increasing the reptile population of the lake some threefold.

'Oh goodness, what ARE we going to do?' gasped Belle as the four, plus Custard, stood huddled together on the centre apex of the fast-dwindling islet, staring at the rising water as though hypnotised.

'Pray,' said Candice. 'They say the Great Ruler in the Sky will always listen to appeals for help from people in desperate straits.'

'What do you think, Uno?' asked Adam hoarsely, as the water once more covered their feet and began to creep up their ankles.

'Miss Candice have good idea, but not time for Divine intervention,' said Uno. He reached into one of the pockets of his waistcoat and extracted a small muslin bag. 'Master say use only in emergency. Emergency now here.' He opened the bag and, as the water began to creep up their legs with a cold and clammy touch that made them gasp for breath, he took out a handful of white powder. He spoke a number of syllables in a tongue none of them had ever heard before and threw the powder into the air. The immediate result was a blinding flash of light just as though a dozen large magnesium flares had been set off simultaneously. They were totally dazed and bedazzled by the sudden violent brightness and could only cling to one another and wait until their eyes had recovered from the shock. When at last they could see again, they stared around them in blank amazement. They were standing in the middle of a clearing in the forest, with a thin transparent mist hovering over them. There were no slopes, no lake, no islet, no alligators (or crocodiles) and no piranha fish. All these had completely vanished, just as had the bound girl and the boat.

Uno met their incredulous gaze with a serious face.

'New powder very efficacious,' he said with great gravity. 'Must compliment master on return home. You agree, pliss?'

Adam was the first to find his voice. 'That ... that powder,' he said with difficulty. 'Castroglio gave it to you?'

'Yes. Master say emergency only. Obeyed. Very good. Must tell master. He like to know it works.'

'You mean it has not been tested before?' Candice asked alertly.

'No.'

'But supposing it had not worked?' Adam gasped.

'It worked,' Uno stated with some surprise. 'What use worry about what might have been, pliss?'

'Very sensible,' commented Candice. 'But, purely as a matter of interest, you understand, why haven't you used it before now? We've had other emergencies – the shark, me in the swamp...'

'They real – powder not work. Lake and contents not real ... powder work,' Uno explained with devastating simplicity.

Candice and Adam were silently thoughtful, reflecting both on their narrow escape and on the marvels of occult science as exemplified by Uno's magical powder. But Belle impulsively went to the dwarf, hugged him, and gave him a kiss on his furry forehead.

'You're wonderful, Uno. Thank you,' she said fervently.

'Not thank me. Thank master.' Uno gently disengaged himself from Belle's embrace. 'We go on, pliss?'

'Yes,' agreed Adam. 'But I'm beginning to wonder just what we're going to meet next. So far it's been one confrontation after the other. I'm losing count of all the problems and dangers we've come across. Can't they leave us alone for just five minutes?'

'I agree,' said Belle with deep sincerity. 'I'm sure my nerves will never be the same after this trip.'

'Oh pish!' said Candice rudely. 'Let 'em all come, I say. We've done all right up till now, haven't we? And we can go on.' She paused, then went on. 'I'm more interested in who or what was responsible for this last happening – all those visions, or whatever they were. No, "visions" isn't the right word. After all, we could FEEL them as well as see them. We rowed the boat to the island, didn't we? We felt the water creep up over our feet, didn't we? Who could conjure up THAT kind of illusion and why?'

'Not know who,' admitted Uno. 'Very strong sorcerer. Impressive display. Maybe Black Baron. But know why – to keep us from castle. They know we come. Not want. They try again. Everyone take much care pliss?'

He picked up his stick and trotted on into the forest again. The others followed, Candice keeping Custard on the lead and Adam once again bringing up the rear.

145

4

It was only some ten minutes later that Uno stopped once again, and stood with his furry head cocked on one side. Once again everyone bumped into the person in front, and once again Adam demanded to know, somewhat peevishly, what was wrong this time.

Uno held up his paw and they stood silent, listening. The sun blazed down from the blue sky and sunlight dappled the track and the bushes on either side; numerous insects whizzed and buzzed and hummed around them. Apart from these noises, everything seemed quiet.

'Is it the watchers again?' asked Candice, keeping her voice low.

'Not seen them. But they follow, keep hidden. Very bad. Not like.'

'I don't fancy being watched either,' said Belle with a shiver. 'It's downright creepy. Who are they and what do they want and why don't they come out into the open?'

'Perhaps they're afraid of us,' suggested Adam.

'Twaddle!' scoffed Candice. 'Why should they be afraid of us? There's probably dozens of them, and only four of us – well, four and a half if you include Custard.'

Hearing his name, the dog looked up from the ground and gave a short yelp, then backed away, tail between his legs, when everyone shushed him.

'Perhaps they're figments of our imagination, like that lake,' suggested Belle tentatively, hoping that she was right, as then Uno might be able to use his magic powder on them.

'If they are, they're figments of Uno's imagination, as I haven't seen or heard anything of them,' responded Adam.

'Not seen or heard,' said Uno calmly. 'KNOW they there.'

'Uno's not the only one,' Candice said quietly. 'I've had my suspicions for some time. In fact, just before we came across that lake – or not-lake, whichever you prefer – I thought I saw one of them flitting through the trees behind us.'

'Why didn't you say anything at the time?' Adam asked.

'Seeing the lake knocked it out of my head,' admitted Candice.

'What could we have done about it anyway?' said Belle reasonably.

Adam had the feeling that the two girls were siding with one another against him, and he didn't like the idea.

'We could have gone up to him and asked him why he was following us,' he said defensively.

'How do you know he would have been able to understand you?' Belle argued. 'And it might not have been a human being, anyway.'

'No point discussing,' said Uno with a trace of disapproval in his reedy voice. 'We go on pliss?'

It was some fifteen minutes later that the great disaster occurred. At the time they were crossing a small cleared space between a couple of giant trees with immensely thick trunks that towered high in the air, soaring up to great masses of dense foliage from which dangled groups of lianas, creepers and vines, some reaching the ground in places. Without any warning there was an unusual swishing noise and the next moment their feet were swept from under them and they were hauled bodily up into the air. It happened so quickly that none of them realised what was going on. They were carried up and up, not knowing whether they were on their head or their heels. When at last the sickening upwards movement ceased, they hung together, swaying about, all mixed up in a higgledy-piggledy heap. Gradually they stopped feeling dizzy and sorted themselves out. It was then that they realised that they were caught up in a large net, high above the ground. They knelt or stood inside the net, clutching hold of the sides and each other, gazing about them and downwards in amazement and terror; Custard staggered around on his paws, not understanding where he was and not liking it one bit, signifying his keen dislike by whining pitifully.

'Galloping groundhogs!' said Candice faintly. 'We've been caught like a shoal of stupid fish!'

The strands of the net were thick, fibrous cords, like hempen rope, and the whole affair hung and swayed some thirty or so metres off the ground, just below the solid greenery of the foliage belonging to the twin giants of the forest that they had spotted a minute or so ago.

'Well and truly caught!' exclaimed Adam in utter disgust.

'Like … like tiddlers in a fishing net,' said Belle in dismay.

'Not good,' said Uno seriously. 'Not like.'

148

'Who's likely to have done this to us?' Candice asked Uno.

'Not known. Maybe Ornithomes, but not heard use nets. Maybe others.'

'That's not especially helpful,' grumbled Adam.

'And how do we get free?' asked Belle desperately.

Adam took out his knife and sawed at one of the thick strands. But after a minute of patient work he gave up. 'Don't know what this stuff is but it won't cut,' he said despondently.

'And if it did, how would you get down?' asked Belle, ever practical.

'Leap onto one of those creepers or vines and slide down,' he said, pointing.

'And supposing it wasn't attached up top, and you fell to the ground?' queried Belle. 'You wouldn't bounce, you know.'

'Well, you're not exactly helping with remarks like that,' he said in an aggrieved voice. 'And if you're so clever, you tell us how to get out of this mess.'

'I wasn't trying to be clever,' snapped Belle.

'Yes you were.'

'No I wasn't.'

'Yes you were.'

'No I wasn't.'

'You were.'

'I wasn't.'

'Were.'

'Wasn't.'

'Were.'

'Wasn't.'

'Oh pooh!' he said feebly, for want of something better to say.

149

'Has it occurred to you two infants that this is neither the time nor the place for bickering?' said Candice wearily, whilst Uno gazed at them with surprised eyes. 'Save your energies for working out how we can get out of this trouble we're in.'

She swarmed lithely up the mesh and hacked with her knife at the top where the thick strands were gathered tightly together, but soon slithered down again.

'No use. I don't know what this stuff is, but my knife won't touch it. Whoever or whatever wove it must be pretty clever.'

Uno examined the strands and tried to cut them with his sword.

'Ordinary hemp, but covered,' he reported. 'Very strong. Secretion from body perhaps. We prisoners. Can do nothing but wait.'

And so they waited, more or less patiently but not for very long.

'Oh crumbs!' ejaculated Adam, as the net shook wildly and Custard barked. 'What's happening now?'

'I think we're on our way down,' gasped Belle.

She was right. As they clutched at the net-strands and peered through the mesh, they saw the massive tree trunks gliding upwards past their eyes, and the distant ground moving towards them. The net descended in a series of jerks and they were thrown about and tossed hither and yon. But eventually they bumped on the grass and the net folded in on them. They struggled to their feet and discovered that the gathering of the strands at the top had slackened and there was now an aperture. Uno and Adam pulled it open and allowed the two girls to escape, then they too scrambled out of the net ... to find themselves totally surrounded by strange beings.

Candice bent down and snatched Custard up into her arms. The four adventurers backed into a compact group and stood gazing nervously at their captors. Afterwards, in an attempt to describe his first impression of the newcomers, Adam had referred to them as 'a bunch of unhappy stick-insects standing upright, everyone at least a metre taller than a human being', which the others agreed was quite good for an off-the-cuff assessment. There were probably some thirty of the creatures round them, all armed with long, thin bamboo poles each tipped with a sharp-pointed flint. All were very tall, and so thin that (as Adam remarked subsequently) each one could have passed through a closed door without opening it. This was a slight exaggeration, but it vividly illustrated the long, narrow bodies, which were virtually transparent so that their pipe-like bones were visible through the thin, lilac-coloured skin and flesh. Their arms and legs were in proportion, the latter terminating in wide, flat feet, the former in big hands with long prehensile fingers. Their heads were small, perched on the top of slender necks, and consisted mostly of a hairless cranium, with two bulging green eyes in the approximate centre of the 'face', a very long, thin proboscis like that of an ant-eater, and – as far as they could see – no mouth. They were vaguely humanoid, but far from human and, although they wore no clothing, there was no evidence of any sexual characteristics, so that one could not tell if they were male or female.

They made no sound, but stood (again, as Adam said later) like a bunch of inanimate and anaemic rhubarb stalks, their huge eyes fixed on their captives, their bodies swaying slightly but otherwise motionless.

'What ... what are they?' whispered Belle in a shaky voice.

'Follow us all time,' answered Uno. 'Species not known. Not Ornithomes – no feathers. Maybe Phasmidomes. Not likely Phyllidomes. Possibly Gryllidomes. Interesting.'

'Interesting they may be,' said Candice with slight impatience. 'But do they mean us harm?'

'Not know. No evidence undue hostility yet.'

'They don't exactly look friendly, either,' opined Adam, striving to appear nonchalant. 'In fact, stringing us up high in the air in a net strikes ME as a very hostile act. But why don't they say something? They're just standing there quivering like matchsticks made out of jelly.'

'No attempt communication – with us or between them,' said Uno. 'Interesting.'

'You mean they can't speak?'

'No oral orifice visible,' explained Uno. 'But such not necessary for communication. Must study more.'

For about five minutes they waited, wondering what was going to happen next. They were afraid to move or speak, and there was no sign of animation from the gathering of stalk-like creatures. But at long last they stirred and, quite suddenly, erupted into vigorous activity, as though moved by a single spring. They began to agitate their thin bodies without actually lifting their feet off the ground, shaking, wavering, oscillating, fluctuating and every other kind of movement. They shook their 'spears', although not so much menacingly as in a ceremonial manner, and their heads rolled from side to side and round and round, until there were strong grounds for fearing that they might fall off. Every one of the creatures present took part, and they acted in total unison, like a well-drilled chorus-line.

Then, just as suddenly, all movement stopped. A moment later, the circle of creatures nearest to the prisoners lifted their weapons and jabbed them forward in a distinctly threatening manner.

'What's up now?' asked Adam hoarsely.

'We go,' replied Uno simply. 'If we no go, we die. So we go, pliss?'

'That makes sense,' agreed Candice.

The ranks of the creatures opened up and Uno led his little band between the rows. Their warders kept up with them once they were on the move and, with several of the stick-insects leading, plenty more on either side and some behind as well – now all shaking their spears in a definitely menacing manner – the four in the centre were escorted willy-nilly through the forest.

5

Despite the fact that they were clearly prisoners, they were allowed to talk freely amongst themselves, but no amount of conjecture or speculation could improve their situation or produce a way of escape from their perilous plight. At one stage Adam did make a tentative movement to break free, but was immediately and decisively dissuaded from his intended course of action by several prods from sharp spears and angry glares from those large, green orb-like eyes.

Eventually they crossed a wooden bridge over what looked like a small canal and arrived at a spacious clearing partly occupied by a number of large objects which, as Adam suggested – and the others agreed – were dwelling places, although they bore little resemblance to normal housing. They were in fact more like giant beehives – tall, narrow, dome-shaped erections about six metres high, constructed of some fibrous material coated in a shiny substance similar to the secretion covering the strands of the net that had been the instrument of their capture. There appeared to be no windows or doors, but each dome had a round opening less than a metre in width and set some two metres above the ground. As they drew nearer, Adam counted some thirty or more of these domes, set in an irregular pattern surrounding a wide central space. There were more of the tall, attenuated creatures moving about in the central space and between the domes, each one seemingly intent on its own purpose; there did not appear to be any contact or communication between them.

Uno gazed about him with bright, inquisitive eyes. 'Strange. Live in community, like primates, yet...'

'I hope they're a bit more civilised than most primates,' said Belle with a shiver.

'Many so-called civilised communities can behave in a most barbarous fashion at times,' said Candice.

Uno nodded. 'Miss Candice speak truth. But these not barbarians.'

'You'd better be right,' Adam said grimly.

They were escorted towards one of the domes situated almost in the centre of the settlement and the motioning of the bamboo spears indicated only too clearly that they should enter. They gazed up at the hole above their head.

'Surely they don't expect us to climb up there?' Belle said with a frown.

The creatures again became agitated, moving their bodies and their heads in unison, but again without any sound. Then one of them came forward, dropped its spear, and sprang upwards, diving effortlessly head-first into the aperture. A moment later it dived out again, landed, bounced back onto its feet and picked up its spear again.

'Well, that was pretty clever!' said Adam admiringly. 'Should we applaud, do you think?'

'I'm wondering if we're expected to do the same,' said Belle with a worried expression. 'I couldn't possibly manage anything like that.'

'Easy!' remarked Candice, and she emulated the

155

creature's lithe spring, leaping up and disappearing head-first through the opening in one agile movement. An instant later her voice came to their ears.

'Come on, you three. I'll be here to catch you.'

'Up you go, Belle,' said Adam. 'Uno and I will give you a bunk-up.'

'Many hands make light work,' said Belle with a shrug. The other two assisted her up the front of the dome and pushed her through the entrance. She vanished inside with a wave of her legs. Adam then went to help Uno up, but the dwarf shook his head. 'Easy for me. I help you.'

Adam felt somewhat chagrined at this remark, because he had to admit to himself that, as far as he could see, it was not as easy as Candice had demonstrated and Uno had decided. But he could not manage it by himself and so allowed Uno to help him up to the hole. He fell through it and was caught by the two girls. By the time he had resumed the perpendicular, Uno had joined them, looking remarkably unruffled. They gazed around them. Light entered through the main opening and also through a number of small holes in the upper sides of the dome revealing that, apart from a flat, earthen floor covered in dry grasses, and the smooth inner walls, there was nothing else. The interior was completely empty.

'Well, here's a fine kettle of fish,' said Belle dejectedly. 'What now, I wonder?'

'Need time to rest, eat, drink,' advised Uno. 'Later we plan escape.'

'Seems a sound suggestion,' agreed Adam, suddenly realising how empty his stomach felt. They searched in their shoulder-bags and pooled their remaining food

156

items, sitting cross-legged on the grassy floor and enjoying their frugal meal. Uno was strangely silent and thoughtful as the others chatted. When they had finished eating, he spoke.

'Beg leave talk. Recall Miss Belle asking how climb to entrance? Recall also creature demonstrating answer? How they know question?'

'They saw us looking puzzled,' replied Adam. 'And Belle spoke to them in a questioning tone of voice.'

'Suggest creatures not understand puzzled look or questioning tone,' objected Uno. 'But they knew question. How?'

'Yes, I can see what you mean,' nodded Candice. 'Were you thinking what I'm thinking?'

'Not know, because not practise telepathy – unlike creatures.'

'Unlike creature,' repeated Belle. 'You mean, they practise telepathy? Mind-reading? I didn't think such things were possible.'

'All things POSSIBLE,' asserted Uno. 'Not so many probable. Telepathy exists. Creatures no speech organs, no wings rub together, no vibrating stomach parts, but communicate. Must use telepathy. Like idea, pliss?'

'I don't know that I like it,' Adam said thoughtfully. 'But it IS an idea, certainly. They seem to have some kind of organisation here, and how can you organise without communication?'

'Profound thought,' nodded Uno, and Adam blushed with pleasure.

'But how does it help us?' queried Belle.

'Miss Belle very practical,' said Uno. 'No answer yet.'

It was clear that Uno was just beginning to warm to his role as mentor, guide and tutor to his three charges, and was blossoming out with personal comments that were – so far – complimentary.

There was a short silence, with everyone obviously thinking about the problem. Custard lay at his mistress's feet, his mournful eyes fixed on her face in case she should see fit to acknowledge his presence with a kind word. But, beyond an occasional absent-minded caress, she paid little attention to him, and eventually he curled up into a small ball and went to sleep.

'We could fight our way out,' Candice said at length, with a warlike expression. 'They don't look all that strong, and we have knives and Uno's sword, and sticks. We ought to be able to give 'em a good run for their money.'

Uno looked puzzled. 'What money?' he asked.

Candice tried to explain. 'I mean we might spring it on 'em as a surprise attack, and get away before they could react.'

'Not good,' replied Uno with a shake of his furry head. 'Possible one or more get hurt. Master not like – punish Uno. Also believe creatures stronger than look.'

'I say, what about your famous powder?' Adam said eagerly. 'It got rid of the lake and the crocs, etcetera. Reckon it's worth a try?'

'Not work on real things,' explained Uno patiently. 'Only imaginings.'

'Imaginings!' cried Adam with delight. 'I like it!'

'Uno, how do you know this settlement isn't one of your "imaginings"?' asked Candice.

Adam got up and banged the sides of the dome with his fist. It gave out a hollow vibrating sound, like the tolling of a big bell.

158

'Feels solid enough,' he commented.

'So did that boat we rowed over to the island,' Candice reminded him.

Uno took out the muslin pouch, extracted some powder, cast it into the air and uttered a selection of unintelligible sounds. Everyone waited tensely.

Nothing happened.

Uno gave a philosophical shrug and put the pouch away.

'Ah well, it was a good idea,' Adam said comfortingly to Candice, hoping that her support of his original idea meant that she thought more highly of his intellect than hitherto.

'No it wasn't,' she said flatly. 'It didn't work. Ideas are only good if they work.'

'What do you think they intend to do with us?' Belle asked Uno, unable to keep the apprehension from her voice.

'Not know. Believe nothing harmful.'

'How can you know that?' Adam challenged him.

'Pardon, master Adam, said believe, not know. Have feeling. Believe picked up creatures' thoughts. Not hostile, more curious. Believe want study us, like ... like...'

'Like specimens under a microscope,' supplied Adam, and groaned. 'Oh fine! I've always wanted to be kept in a bottle, or pinned to a card. You don't think they might want to take us to pieces to see how we work, do you?'

'Oh Adam, don't,' wailed Belle.

'Not be concerned, pliss,' said Uno quickly. 'Master Adam joke, no?'

'Master Adam joke, yes,' said Adam quickly to reassure Belle.

'I must say I don't exactly share your touching faith in these gawky monsters, Uno,' said Candice sceptically. 'I suggest we plan our escape just as soon as we can.'

'I second that,' agreed Belle.

'Not move too soon,' warned Uno. 'Plan – yes. Not move yet. Creatures suspicious, keep eye on us. Wait until suspicion fades, then move, pliss?'

'If you say so,' said Candice grumpily, and spoke no more. Adam wondered if she had gone off into a sulk, because she didn't talk again for quite a while, despite the fact that the rest of them indulged in a lively discussion on ways and means of escape. Unfortunately they had virtually no information on their captors' habits and customs, nor of the precise layout of the thirty or so domes, so they were somewhat hampered by lack of meaningful data and came to no useful conclusions.

Evening descended swiftly and, when the daylight had entirely vanished and they sat in darkness, Adam lifted Belle up to the aperture so that she could cling to the lower lip and look around for anything that might be useful. To their dismay she reported that the entire settlement was now brightly lit by a series of torches fastened to long poles stuck in the ground at strategic intervals, each one providing a flaring, flickering light that populated the domes and the tracks and spaces between them with dancing agitated shadows. There was also a ring of small fires extending right round the perimeter of the settlement, whilst between them, here and there, stood creatures, spears at the ready, silent and watchful sentinels. Other creatures moved around along the tracks and between the domes just as they had done earlier, whilst one of the domes

160

– larger than the others – seemed to have two large apertures high up on its front, and creatures dived in and out of these two holes from time to time. Belle reported that a kind of one-way system was in operation, one hole for entry, one hole for exit. It appeared that there was no reduction or cessation of activity just because night had fallen.

'Don't they ever sleep?' groaned Adam as he lowered Belle to earth and rubbed his aching muscles.

'Maybe not sleep,' suggested Uno.

'Not sleep!' echoed Adam. 'How can they possibly go without sleep?'

'Easily,' answered Candice. 'I can will myself to stay awake all night if I want to. Perhaps these creatures can as well.'

'Maybe not sleep ever,' added Uno. 'Different species, different ways. Most need sleep renew strength; maybe these have other ways do same thing. You like, pliss?'

'No,' grunted Adam. 'If they're like that, it's going to make it ten times more difficult to escape. I only hope you're wrong.'

The discussion continued for a while, but it was all to no avail and, since they needed rest even if the creatures didn't (with the possible exception of Candice), it was not long before they had all emulated Custard and had gone to sleep curled up on the floor of the dome.

6

Adam returned to consciousness with a sudden start, aware firstly of a hand pressing his shoulder, and secondly of a confused and noisy commotion outside the dome. He sat up and rubbed his eyes. A flickering light filtered in through the small opening high up in the dome wall, and he saw Belle stirring nearby. There was a figure up at the opening, clinging to the lower edge and staring out. The hand pressed his shoulder again and he turned to see Candice peering at him through the gloom.

'Wake up,' she whispered. 'Something's happening outside.'

'Like what?' he whispered back as he got to his feet.

'Trouble of some sort. Uno's having a look. What is it, Uno?'

'Trouble correct,' the bear-like dwarf said, dropping lightly to the floor of the dome. 'Settlement under attack. Creatures and enemy fight.'

'Who IS the enemy?' Belle asked, having joined them.

'Not know. Look like metal beings. Very strong, but slow. Have swords.'

'Metal beings?' blinked Adam. 'You mean ... robots? This I must see for myself. Candice, give me a lift up like you did Uno.'

'I didn't give him a lift up,' she replied. She looked

162

at Uno accusingly. 'You got up there all by yourself, didn't you? And you never told us!'

'No one asked,' said the dwarf simply.

'Hold on!' exclaimed Adam. 'You mean he jumped up? Well, I'll go to the foot of our stairs! That's quite a fair jump for a littl'un.' He turned to Candice. 'But it's nothing to get excited about. I can jump almost my own height.'

'He didn't jump,' Candice replied shortly. 'He levitated.'

'He ... he levi ... levitated!' Adam articulated, whilst Belle stared blankly. 'You ... you mean he ... he flew up to the hole?'

'He didn't fly. He floated up, just high enough to be able to grab hold of the sill. And he floated down again – didn't you see him do that?'

'I did, but I didn't take much notice,' confessed Adam. 'But, now you mention it...'

He stopped speaking as something struck the dome. It must have been something heavy, because it resulted in a loud, tolling boom, and the dome shook. They became aware that the conflict had intensified outside. The noises of battle – the clang of metal on metal, the thud of sword against shield, the swish of weapons flying through the air, the shouts and groans and screams – came from all sides and all directions.

Adam made a tremendous leap up, caught the lower rim of the opening and hauled himself up so that he could see out. It was a noteworthy but frightening spectacle that met his eyes. The flaring flames from the torches and the ring of bonfires threw a lurid glow on the hordes of struggling combatants, creating a phantasmagoria of frenzied shapes and agitated shadows. The

163

tall stick-creatures were locked in battle with their opponents who, as far as Adam could tell, were clad in metal armour and wielded long curved swords. It was hard, ruthless, hand-to-hand combat. In every pathway between the domes, and beyond them, pairs of antagonists fought desperately, sword and shield against spear and shield, dark shadows locked in fierce strife, accompanied by thuds and clangs and gasps and grunts.

He dropped back to the ground, eyes alight with excitement.

'Now's our chance to escape!' he exclaimed. 'Now, whilst they're all busy knocking seven bells out of one another. Come on!'

'Are you sure it's safe?' questioned Belle apprehensively.

'No,' admitted Adam. 'But it's not going to get any safer. Agreed, Uno?'

'Believe now better than later,' nodded Uno.

'Candice?'

'No point in hanging around,' replied Candice, who was clearly chafing at the bit and anxious for some action. 'Let's do it. And I'll go first, to make sure everything's clear.'

Before anyone could argue with her, she had leapt up to the opening and pulled herself through. A moment later her voice floated back to them. 'Someone pass Custard out, please.' The dog was duly handed out to her and as she caught him and popped him in her bag, she called out, 'All clear ... come on out.'

Adam and Uno hoisted Belle up to the aperture and helped her through. Then Uno gave Adam a boost and he followed. As he picked himself up off the ground,

Uno came through the opening and floated down to join them. Then they dodged round a pair locked in mortal combat and slipped into the dark shadow of an adjacent dome.

'Bless me – it was easier than I expected,' breathed Belle.

'We're not away yet!' Candice pointed out. As if to underline her statement, one of the stick-creatures spotted them and lifted its spear to hurl it at them. But, before it could let go, it was attacked by one of the armoured beings and had to defend itself. But a second later a spear sailed through the air and clanged against a dome just by Candice's head, whilst an armoured being lumbered towards Adam with its sword raised, only to be tripped up by Uno.

'Let's get away from here!' gasped Candice, and the four of them ran as swiftly as they could towards the ring of bonfires that marked the periphery of the settlement. As they rushed along, a spear was hurled at them and dug into the ground near Belle, and they had to leap over one of the stick-creatures that had been felled, and now lay still and apparently lifeless.

They weaved between the domes, skilfully avoiding groups of combatants who fortunately were too engrossed in their battles to bother about the fugitives, and finally arrived at the boundary, only to find their way barred by what looked like a moat filled with water. It was about six metres across and looked very deep.

'Oh crumbs!' said Adam blankly, staring at it. 'I didn't expect this.'

'Crossed bridge on way to settlement,' Uno reminded him. 'This part of settlement defences.'

'So how do we get across?' asked Belle, still breathless from the headlong flight from the village.

'Easy – jump,' said Candice confidently.

'All that distance?' Belle gasped.

'Well, we've got to get across somehow,' said Adam. 'Uno, what about your levitation act – will that work?'

'Not across, only up and down. And what about rest of party?'

'Oh come on!' exclaimed Candice impatiently. 'Those who are too feeble to jump can swim.'

With that she retreated a few paces, gathered her strength and then raced to the edge, launching herself into the air. She landed safely on the further side with knees bent, then bounced upright and turned.

'Told you it would be easy,' she said in triumph.

'Golly!' said Belle inadequately. Inside, she was not only jealous of the older girl's agility, but furious that Candice had shown up her – Belle's – physical ineptitude.

'If you can't manage it, you'll have to swim,' Adam told her.

She nodded forlornly. But at that moment Candice gave a shout and pointed towards the settlement, where flames were now leaping up from burning domes and smoke drifted across the battlefield. Amid the conflagration, fighting was still in progress, distant bunches of warriors and stick-creatures, half-hidden by the smoke, striking at one another with their weapons. From one nearby area a small group of armoured soldiers were clumping awkwardly but purposefully towards them, waving their swords in a threatening manner.

'Oh bless me!' wailed Belle. 'Out of the frying pan into the fire.'

Uno pushed her and Adam towards the edge of the moat.

'Join Miss Candice, pliss. I stop them catching you.'

He drew his sword and was about to head towards the oncoming enemy when Adam grasped his arm.

'No you don't, Uno. You'll be killed. We've got to stick together. Agreed, Belle?'

'Yes, yes!' cried Belle, near to tears at the thought of what might happen to the furry little creature.

'Hurry!' shouted Candice from the other side of the water, but then she gave a shriek as three armoured beings converged on her from the darkness. She drew her knife and prepared to defend herself, but a swift lunge from a long sword disarmed her, and the next instant she was seized and held captive.

'That's it then,' remarked Belle with a philosophical shrug. 'We're caught.'

Uno turned on hearing the shriek from Candice and, when he saw that she had been made captive, he sheathed his sword. The next moment the small group of the enemy had reached him and secured him, and within minutes Belle and Adam were similarly pinioned. They were disarmed, their shoulder-bags were taken from them and they were marched round the periphery of the village and away from the scene of the fighting, which had now largely finished. They were forced across the bridge to join Candice and her captors. She had clearly been handled very roughly: her animal-skin costume was torn and she looked very crestfallen indeed. Once they were all together, the leader of the group raised the visor on his helmet and exposed a red and brutal face that was undeniably human.

'You're coming with us,' he said, his harsh voice

167

throbbing with triumph. 'We've been keeping a watch on you ever since you landed on the island. When our spies reported that the Stalks had captured you and were holding you prisoner in their village, we decided that the time had come for us to liberate you.' He guffawed loudly, then turned to his followers. 'That's right, lads, ain't it? We've come here specially to rescue them. Ain't we the kindhearted ones, eh? Haw, haw!'

There were several guffaws in return, but Adam noticed that only two out of the six henchmen showed any inclination to agree with their leader; the rest remained silent and showed no reaction whatsoever. He wondered if this indicated that most of the group were perhaps disenchanted with their leader and might possibly help the captives to escape. It was an intriguing thought.

'Come on!' snapped the leader, jerking at Uno. 'My master wants to have a word with you lot.'

'Who is your master?' asked Adam as the armoured men escorted them away from the bridge.

'Who? WHO? Why, none other than the Black Baron of Xakkara, that's who,' said the leader, and guffawed again when he saw the momentary look of alarm in the other's eyes. 'Aye, I thought that'd make you squirm! But it ain't nothing to how you'll squirm later, my beauties!'

'Where does he live?' asked Belle, who remembered what Castroglio had told them, but wanted to hear it from one of his own men. The leader gazed at her incredulously.

'You've landed here on his island and you don't know that!' he jeered. 'You want to watch out, young 'un – he eats little girls like you for breakfast!' Another guffaw. 'But, in case you're all more stupid than I think you are, I'll tell you. He lives in the Castle Grimaldi, and that's where we're taking you right now.'

The four prisoners and the dog were forced to climb up into a covered wagon drawn by four animals that looked like horses but were squat and massive like hooded oxen. Guarded by several silent figures in armour, the captives were driven, with shouts and frequent cracks of a whip, away from the settlement and through a dark land that was not yet tinged with the approach of dawn. Seated inside the wagon, they could hear the rattle of hooves on the rough track, the snorting and grunting from the animals, and the rumble of the huge wheels as the wagon jolted and swayed and bounced over the appalling highway towards their destination.

'Great leaping llamas!' ejaculated Candice, as one particularly violent jolt sent her to the floor on her back. 'What's the hurry?'

No one replied. Adam was deeply depressed at the turn of events and was preoccupied by wondering what fate awaited them inside the Castle. Belle seemed to have been deprived of her usual spirit by their plight; and Uno was uncommunicative. Even Custard had lain where Candice had deposited him, under one of the wooden benches inside the wagon, not making a sound. Eventually the blonde girl got up and resumed her seat without further comment.

The vehicle continued to sway and rock as it climbed a winding track up the hill, but from the back the prisoners could see only darkness, and wreaths of phantom mist drifting in to fill the vacuum left by their onward rush. Then the sounds made by the pounding hooves and the rumbling wheels changed as they were driven through a huge gateway and over a bridge across a moat. The gates clanged shut behind them and they drove through a second archway, the great doors of which closed behind them with a sound of thunder as they careered on into an extensive courtyard surrounded by high granite walls.

PART FOUR

THE CASTLE

1

The Castle was huge, dark and forbidding. It squatted astride a stark hill like a gargantuan petrified toad, and was entirely surrounded by high stone walls and a deep moat. It was built of enormous granite slabs and was thus tremendously strong, with narrow slits in the walls that were easy to fire from but almost impossible to fire into. There was a drawbridge across the moat leading to a great arched entrance in which were set two massive doors of immense thickness and weight. There were towers and battlements; buttresses and turret; innumerable halls and chambers and rooms on every floor; giant stone staircases and flights of stone steps winding around colossal stone pillars; dark corridors leading hither, thither and yon; small octagonal cells in the turrets and towers; gloomy cavernous dungeons below ground; and secret rooms and hidden staircases and concealed passages. The roofs of the Castle were many and steep, covered in ancient tiles that were sunken and moss-encrusted, at all angles and all heights, pierced by dozens of small dormer windows and skylights and ornamented by tall, twisted chimneys. The peaked roofs, high turrets and tall chimneys were populated by birds during the day, and bats at night, whilst the kilometres of passages and the innumerable rooms were infested with rodents and insects and slimy things too horrible to mention. Even with the sun on

173

it, and a blue sky overhead, the Castle presented a dark and sinister appearance; at night, with a stormy cloud-scape surging nervously across a black sky, and a gibbous moon occasionally spilling its leprous light through the cumulo-nimbus, and the pale, ghostly mist that eternally wreathed the Cyclopean edifice, the Castle loomed over the dark landscape like a harbinger of dreadful doom. It was a grim, monstrous building fit only to preside over Hell itself.

Once the huge doors to the courtyard had been closed, the animals were reined in to a snorting hoof-clattering halt, the wagon wheels ceased to turn, and armoured soldiers lumbered across to stand guard and to prevent the prisoners escaping. Dull yellow light filtered through the narrow slits in the thick walls to cast oblong patches of colour on the uneven cobblestones. The leader dismounted from his steed and strode round to the rear of the wagon to sneer at them.

'Wait here,' he growled. 'Make just one move to escape and you'll all die, make no mistake about that!'

His boots grated on the cobbles as he departed towards a door at the base of one of the towering granite walls. The four inside the wagon looked at one another with dejection on their faces.

'I'm ... I'm afraid,' said Belle with a slight quiver in her voice. 'I'm afraid of what they'll do to us. Adam...'

'There's nothing we can do at the moment,' said Adam, trying to speak in a reassuring voice. He looked at the guards standing sentinel with their visors down. 'Those swords of theirs look a bit too sharp for my

174

taste. We shall just have to bide our time and see what develops.'

'If we wait much longer it'll be too late,' said Candice sharply. 'Once they get us into a cell – and I'm certain that's what they'll do to us next – we might never get out.'

Adam felt this to be a rebuke for his lack of backbone and was goaded into exclaiming, 'Alright, clever-clogs; if you're so smart, tell us how to overcome these guards without us getting carved up, and then how to find our way out of the Castle and we'll do it.'

'I didn't mean this very minute, stupid!' retorted Candice. 'I meant … well, on the way to the dungeons, for instance.'

'You reckon they're going to let us walk there on our own?' enquired Adam with what he hoped was withering sarcasm.

'No I don't – I'm not quite as stupid as you seem to think I am,' Candice retaliated. 'But there may be a moment on the way – like when we're turning a corner, for instance, or passing an open doorway – when we might be able to break free and make a run for it. We've got to seize whatever chances are offered to us.'

'Idea good,' interposed Uno. 'Dungeons where we want be – good they take us there.'

'That sounds fine,' agreed Belle. 'Much better than wrangling amongst ourselves like little children.'

'Who's wrangling like little children?' Adam demanded aggressively.

'You and Candice.'

'No we're not.'

'Yes you are.'

'We're not.'

175

'You are.'

'We're...'

This juvenile, and by now familiar, exchange between them was mercifully cut short by the reappearance of the leader. His visor was still raised and his face was, if possible, even more red and brutal than before. He glowered at them.

'You're lucky,' he growled. 'The master can't see you now. Perhaps tomorrow. So you get to live a bit longer.' He guffawed at his own crude jest. 'So for now we're going to put you where you won't be able to cause any trouble. Come on!'

'To the dungeons?' Adam asked hopefully as they were escorted across the cobbled courtyard towards a stone archway, Candice clutching Custard to her bosom.

'No, lad. We've got dozens of Stalk prisoners coming in and they've got to be put down there.' The leader saw their faces change and he guffawed once more. 'Has that upset your little plan for escape? Haw haw!' Then his grin changed to a scowl. 'No, we're putting you in one of the top turret rooms. You'll have no chance of escaping from those places – unless you can fly, of course!' A further guffaw ended his speech.

They looked at one another disconsolately. This latest catastrophic piece of news reduced their spirits to a very low ebb, and they saw no way out. But worse was yet to come. Any ideas they may have had of trying to escape during their transfer from the wagons was knocked on the head when each one had his or her wrists bound behind them, the leader grabbing the dog from Candice so that she could receive the same treatment. As he held the struggling, whining animal, she gave him a deadly look.

176

'You harm that dog and I swear I'll kill you for it,' she hissed.

'You'll kill no one, girl,' he snarled. Then, to their surprise, his voice softened. 'I don't aim to harm it, child. I just do what I'm told. Now get going, and no more backchat.'

Thus pinioned, they had no option but to shuffle after the leader, escorted by half-a-dozen beings in armour and carrying flaring torches. Each one wore a sword, and moved stiffly, almost as if the armour was too heavy for him.

The prisoners were made to climb a flight of stone steps that wound upwards round an enormously thick pillar composed of granite slabs. The steps went up and up and up, and round and round and round, until they were breathless and dizzy; they could only imagine that they must be near the very topmost level of the Castle. Finally the steps ended at a long corridor, which they were forced to traverse. Another flight of steps followed, running straight this time: more corridors, more stairs, and finally a set of wooden steps, angled steeply upwards, that led to a small landing. There were passages leading off through archways on either side, and a door in the farthest wall. One of the torches was slid into an iron bracket fastened to the wall to provide light. The leader stepped up to the door, moved aside a small panel, and peered into the room. Satisfied, he drew back and signed to one of his men, who clumped forward, drew back thick, rusty bolts top and bottom (each of which moved with a protesting squeak) and hauled the door open. The rest of the armoured soldiers seized the prisoners and thrust them over the threshold.

As Candice stumbled forward into the darkened chamber, she shouted, 'What about our bonds?' But all she received for an answer was a jeering laugh. Custard was pushed in after them and the door slammed shut. The bolts squeaked loudly again as they were thrust home. The leader's red face appeared in the small opening.

'You lot think you're so clever, so you can have fun untying the ropes yourselves,' he said, guffawed yet once more (it was beginning to get on their nerves) and closed the panel with a click. They heard a sharp word of command, followed by the tramp of heavy boots going down the wooden stairs. The sounds died away, and then they were left in silence and in darkness.

2

There was a short pause, then Adam said, 'Crumbs, but it's dark in here. I suppose no one's got a light?'

'I haven't,' responded Candice. 'Haven't you?'

'I wouldn't have asked if I had,' retorted Adam. 'Uno?'

'No light.'

'What about that powder stuff of your master's – likely to be any good?'

'No good.'

'Belle?'

'No, I'm sorry, Adam, I haven't.'

There was a noise from somewhere within the chamber, indicative of someone or something moving, then a voice said, 'I've got one.'

The voice was unfamiliar, and startled them with its unexpectedness. It sounded boyish, belonged to someone male but not all that old, and it came from a corner of the room.

A long silence ensued, broken eventually by Adam, in a voice sharpened by surprise and apprehension. 'Who was that?'

'There's someone in here with us,' exclaimed Candice, and Custard roused himself sufficiently to bark out loud.

'Wh … who's speaking?' quavered Belle, her voice very unsteady.

A feeble illumination sprang into being in the corner, flickered, wavered, then brightened. It came from a small lamp held by someone who sat against the wall. The lamp was so constructed that the light was concentrated into a beam that travelled across the floor and came to rest on their faces, one by one. When it reached Belle, it stopped, and the holder of the lamp gave a gasp of discovery.

'Sis! It IS you! I thought I recognised your voice, but I just couldn't believe...'

Belle started, her eyes large with amazement. She stammered 'It's ... it's not ... not...'

'Yes, Sis. It's really me – Damon!'

The beam of the lamp was turned onto the face of the holder and they saw that it was a youth, aged somewhere between fifteen and sixteen, reclining at ease on the floor. He was clad in rough and grimy trousers, shirt and sandals. His eyes were a wary blue, his hair black and curly, his chin resolute. His face was pale and drawn, and there was a bad bruise on one cheek, and a cut over one eye, but he was grinning cheerfully. Adam recognised him as the owner of the face in the picture carried by Belle.

'Oh Damon!' sobbed Belle, and she stumbled across the floor and fell on him. 'I've found you, I've found you at last!'

'Why, you're all tied up!' said the youth. He turned her round and in a trice had removed the cords that bound her wrists. Then they embraced and hugged and held one another tightly, and all the others looked away tactfully. But after a reasonable while Adam said, 'When you two have QUITE finished, we'd rather like our ropes off as well.'

180

'Yes, of course,' said the youth at once and scrambled up off the floor. As he untied them, Belle said, in a trembling voice, 'This ... this is Damon, my ... my brother.'

'We guessed that one,' said Candice rather drily.

'He's the one I came all this way to ... to find,' went on Belle. 'And now I've done it. Oh Damon, isn't that marvellous!'

'It's something to marvel about that you and your friends got thrown into the very room I'm in,' replied her brother, who was evidently a calm and prosaic sort of fellow. 'And it would be even MORE marvellous if we weren't all prisoners. And that's something we can all talk about in due course, but first, Belle, you'd better introduce me to all these nice people and especially that smashing little dog over there.'

'He's mine,' said Candice, with a mixture of pride of ownership and pleasure at Damon's compliment.

Belle was still somewhat overcome by her emotions, so Adam did the honours with regard to introductions. Damon's eyes passed over them during Adam's monologue, and lingered for more than a few seconds on Candice. But it was to Uno that he spoke.

'So you're Castroglio's number one! How come I didn't get to meet you when I called on him some two months ago?'

'Away visiting sick relative,' explained Uno.

'Seems reasonable,' admitted Damon. He looked at Adam and Candice.

'But what are you all doing HERE, and how did you get here?'

'Come to think of it, how did YOU get here?' countered Adam.

Damon chuckled.

'Let's strike a bargain,' he said cheerfully. 'First Belle can tell me how SHE got here, and you three can tell me how YOU got here, and then I'll tell you how I got here. Fair enough?'

It appeared it was, and whilst Belle told her brother how she had decided to come in search of him, the others inspected the chamber by the light of Damon's lamp. It was an octagonal room, with a small window-slit in every wall (except for the one containing the door) and a steeply-peaked octagonal ceiling. The floor was raw timber, innocent of any covering, and there was no furniture. Adam decided that it was about as bare as the dome from which they had so recently escaped. But what was far worse was that it was located high up at the very top of the Castle, with possibly as much as a fifty-metre drop from the windows. Adam's heart sank as he began to appreciate how difficult it was going to be to escape. A cloud of despondency settled on him, and through it he heard Damon say to his sister, 'But how did you know where I was?'

'I didn't – not until Mr Castroglio told me you might be here.'

'Before that, I mean. When you left home, how did you know to go into the forest and head north? Why didn't you go south ... east ... west? What prompted you to come in what turned out to be the right direction?'

Belle bit her lips, then blurted out, 'I ... I just knew, that's all. I knew somehow it was the right way. I knew when I started out, and when we entered the Mountain, and afterwards.'

'But how?'

182

Belle did not meet his eyes as she muttered, 'I don't know, I tell you. I just did.'

'But you MUST know!'

'I don't, I don't, I don't!' cried Belle, near to tears.

'Here, there's no need to go on at her like that!' Adam said angrily.

Damon looked at him intently, then grinned.

'Sorry, old lad. Didn't know you were the boyfriend.'

Adam opened his mouth to deny this with some vehemence, but caught sight of Belle's pink face, and for some unaccountable reason felt unable to speak. Uno then entered the conversation.

'Telepathy. Like stick-creatures. Minds in contact over distance. Proven exist. Even I able pick up creature's thoughts.' He stared at Belle with large eyes. 'You and brother. Minds in contact. Like creatures, only you not know. But know now. Good. Work with brother, develop ability. Very good, pliss?'

It was probably the longest speech Uno had made up till now and all were duly impressed.

'I told you,' Candice said to Belle.

'I'm not sure I believe it's true, despite what Uno says,' Belle said defensively. 'Sorry, Uno! I'm not saying you're wrong generally, only in my case. I somehow can't believe that I've been singled out...'

'Others have,' replied Candice. 'Why not you?'

'As YOU might say, Belle, there are more things in heaven than earth, Horatio...' added Adam.

'Well, I believe him,' said Damon, nodding seriously. 'He could be right. We'll have to experiment, see if it's true. If it is, it could come in VERY useful. Anyway, you'd better carry on with your story.'

Belle continued with her long tale, the others

interrupting now and again to add details, to correct minor errors, or to jog her memory about small incidents. The only one who didn't join in was Custard, who – after having had a really good sniff around the newcomer – had clearly accepted him as one of the party, and had curled up near him and fallen asleep. When Belle completed her account, Damon looked at her with admiration.

'Golly, Sis, I didn't know you had it in you! Congratulations!' He stuck out his hand and she shook it, colouring with pleasure. Damon looked at the others. 'And thanks to you all for helping her – I doubt if she'd have made it all on her own.'

'Don't worry about that,' said Candice, whose glances in his direction did not lack favour. 'Let's hear all about you now.'

'Well, I think we should hear from Belle's boyfriend next,' replied Damon. He turned his blue eyes on Adam. 'You're on next, old lad.'

It didn't take Adam long to relate his original reason for making the journey, and how that aim had been changed by the discussion with Castroglio and the information that the sorcerer had imparted.

'So, you see, I'm here to contact this man – the Lord of the Treasury – that Castroglio mentioned,' Adam concluded. 'I'm hoping he can give me some evidence that will enable me to clear my father's name. That's all I want.' He looked curiously at Damon. 'Incidentally, what DID you do to that dwarf from the hollow tree early on in the Forest? He swelled up like a balloon with rage just on seeing your picture.'

'I asked him a question he couldn't answer.'

'What was that?'

184

'Well, since he lived in a tree, I asked him what tree has a foot but no root.'

'What's the answer?'

'A shoe-tree. He got so angry because he didn't know the answer that he blew up like a balloon, just as he did with you. In fact, I was so afraid he'd float away and get lost that I tethered him to his tree. It seems from what you say that he got free, but I wonder how long it took him!'

'No wonder he was so angry,' said Belle, laughing reproachfully.

'Let's hear about you now,' said Candice impatiently, sitting quite close to Damon, ostensibly to scratch Custard's ear but at the same time regarding him with unfeigned interest.

'Won't take long,' said Damon ruefully. 'After your heroic little sagas, my experiences seem very humdrum. Judging by what Sis has said, I must have had all the luck on my side. I missed most of the dangers you encountered. Oh, there were a few adventures – none worth repeating now. They'll keep until later. Actually, my luck ran out when I reached the Island of Jade. I was heading inland when I was spotted by a patrol of those fellows from the Castle. Normally I could have out-run them easily; you've probably noticed how slow they are. But as I was crossing a wide stream by leaping from boulder to boulder, I trod on the head of a crocodile which took exception to my intrusion (naturally enough) and moved rather smartly, thus throwing me into the water. As I fell I hit my head on another boulder, which didn't do me a lot of good! I managed to get out of the stream, but was caught on the bank by the patrol. I was brought here and I've been here ever since. They threw me into the dungeons at first and I was there quite a time, but a few days ago I was transferred up here – no reason given.'

'Reason known – dungeons wanted for other prisoners,' said Uno.

'The Stalks, you mean? Poor devils!' said Damon soberly. 'I wonder why the Black Baron has decided to make war on them. There's always some kind of strife going on here, but of late there's been a sort of armed truce. My sympathies are with the Stalks.'

'Why have you been kept a prisoner for so long?' Adam asked him.

'Presumably because they didn't want to let me go free.'

'But they could've...' Adam paused, suddenly reluctant to voice his thoughts, but Damon had no such qualms.

'Killed me off, you were going to say?'

'Well ... yes.'

'No idea. Just another question we may never know the answer to. But just now we've got more important things to think about, haven't we?'

'Like planning our escape,' said Candice eagerly.

'Yes. But I warn you: I'm not leaving the Castle without the Chalice.'

This bold statement caused a minor sensation. The others stared at him in amazement, which in Belle's case was mixed with deep dismay.

'You too, Damon?' she said, her face a picture of consternation. 'But you CAN'T!'

'Why not? It's what I came all this way for.'

'But it's stealing,' expostulated Adam, righteously

186

indignant, and all the more so because he had been persuaded to renounce the same idea.

'Is it?'

'Yes it is!'

'Who said so?'

'Well Castroglio for one,' said Adam, a trifle lamely.

'He doesn't know everything, despite his crystal ball.' Damon looked round at them and noted their expressions, which ranged from alarm to disapproval. Only Uno remained impassive. Damon's face grew defiant. 'Look, is it stealing to take back what was stolen in the first place?'

'But the Chalice belongs to the High Priests of Zaire,' wailed Belle.

'Right! And THEY are the very people who have commissioned me to steal back the Chalice for them.'

'Commissioned you!' gasped Belle.

'I didn't just dream up the idea of coming here, Sis,' said Damon, enjoying the furore his words were creating. 'You know me – I've always been a bit of a rolling stone, ready for any kind of adventure. The word got around and one day I was approached by a spokesman for the High Priests of Zaire to win back their Chalice. I decided to have a go. It sounded interesting and the pay was good. But I wasn't able to tell you, Sis. In fact, I wasn't able to tell anyone – the Priests didn't want it known that they were prepared to go to such drastic lengths to regain their property.'

'I'm surprised Mr Castroglio didn't know,' said Belle. 'If he's so clever, why didn't he see that in his crystal ball?'

Damon laughed. 'He DID! He knew all about my mission. I persuaded him to keep it dark and he agreed.'

'You very persuasive,' said Uno, looking at Damon admiringly. 'My master not agree to such request easily.'

'You're right!' nodded Damon ruefully. 'He took a lot of convincing.'

'So why are you telling us?' demanded Adam, trying to stifle feelings of jealousy over Damon's suddenly-acquired status as a buccaneer.

'Because I'm counting on you to help me,' replied Damon confidently. 'I reckon that, between us, we can escape from this room, get down to the dungeons, steal the Chalice and get clear away. Let's band together, all for one and one for all, united we stand, divided we fall, two heads are better than one, many hands make light work, all that sort of thing. Are we on?'

Adam wondered what it was about the family of which Belle and Damon were members that they doted so on proverbs.

'You know whereabouts Chalice?' Uno asked Damon.

'I know which dungeon it's in – I found that out when I was down there.'

'And what about the Guardian?' Candice asked bluntly.

Damon gave a wry grimace.

'I never found out about that,' he admitted. 'But I heard it often. It's something pretty colossal and unutterably ferocious, judging by the deep roars I could hear. I gather no one's ever entered its abode and lived to tell the tale.'

'So how exactly do you propose to steal the Chalice?' enquired Adam tartly. 'Tiptoe past this fearsome monster when it's not looking?'

'We'll think of something,' said Damon, still confident. 'Don't you worry. We'll snatch it right from under their

188

noses and be away from here before you can say Mulligatawny soup.'

'NOT until I've had my talk with the Lord of the Treasury,' Adam said with quiet determination.

'H'm – now you're being difficult! Well, we'll have to see what we can do for you.'

'You don't have to do anything for me,' retorted Adam. 'You do what you've come here to do, and I'll do what I've come here to do, and if we can work together so much the better, and if we can't then we go our own ways.'

'Adam!' exclaimed Belle, dismayed at seeing those she obscurely felt were the two men in her young life at loggerheads. 'Let's not quarrel about it. We've got to work together, to help one another, just as Damon said.'

'Yes, but he wants me to help him, not him help me,' said Adam aggrievedly, and with not too much regard for grammar.

The three of them bickered more or less amicably for a while, but eventually they were brought back to reality by a small but resonant snore from Uno. They looked round, to find the remainder of the party (including the dog) fast asleep on the bare floor. Belle and Adam realised then how tired they were, and they too joined their comrades in slumber. Damon propped himself against the wall and pondered on escape plans.

3

When they awoke again, a bright sun was slanting slim dust-laden shafts of warm golden light through some of the window-slits, and Damon was sitting near them eating bread off a wooden platter and drinking from a wooden bowl. Custard stood by him, lapping water from a tray, and Adam realised that it had been the sound of the lapping tongue that had woken him up.

'Come and get it,' Damon said cheerfully, as he noted their return to consciousness. 'Only one meal a day here, so you'd better get over here fast and grab your share before this voracious animal woofs it all up.'

'Do you like dogs?' Candice asked him as they all sat together.

'Dote on 'em,' replied Damon. 'Even gluttonous little beasts like this one. He gobbles his food like a ravenous rhinoceros.'

He dodged a playful punch from Candice and chuckled boisterously.

The fare was basic and not especially palatable – thick slices of dark brown bread spread with some unrecognisable greasy substance, and a jug of water. But they were all very hungry and thirsty and between them they finished it all off.

'How did this little lot appear?' asked Adam, chewing on the hard bread.

'Pushed through that small opening in the base of

190

the door. It's not exactly the sort of service I'm accustomed to but then beggars can't be choosers.'

Adam stared at the opening. It was about twelve centimetres square and was covered on the outside by a board.

'Can it be opened this side?' he asked.

'Possibly. It just slides. Unless, of course, it's fastened on the other side, but I shouldn't think so. On the other hand, unless friend Castroglio came up with a spell to reduce you down to the size of good old Custard here, I don't see how that's going to help.'

Uno rose, scurried across to the opening and pressed his furry paws to the board. It slid open, disclosing the bare floorboards of the landing beyond. He got down onto his plump belly and peered through. Then he got up again and peered out of the window-slits adjacent to the door. After that he studied the slit to the right of the door. Finally, he turned and surveyed the rest of the party, all of whom (with the exception of Custard) had been watching his little performance with deep interest.

'Anyone able pass through window?' he asked, indicating the slit he had just been examining.

'That tiny space?' ejaculated Adam. 'No chance. It can't be more than twenty centimetres wide. And even if one of us could, so what? There's a drop down there that makes me shiver just to think of it.'

'Miss Belle?' persisted the dwarf, turning his eyes onto her.

She went pale then walked slowly over to the window-slit and measured it with her eye. She licked her lips. 'I ... I might ... just about. I ... I don't know...'

'Could – without garments,' Uno said impassively.

191

Belle blushed.

'Oh … no … no I couldn't,' she said hurriedly, going pink.

'Could,' he insisted. 'No one look. Could get out window.'

'But, what then?' she wailed. 'What would I have to do then?'

'This window overlook passage to landing. Window in passage. If cross space between, reach landing, undo bolts.'

Belle stared at him with something like horror, her modesty overwhelmed by a new and far greater fear.

'Oh no no! Not possible. It's … it's so far down! I'd fall – I'm terrible at heights. I'd get dizzy and I'd … I'd fall…'

'Not with rope attached.'

Whilst Belle continued to boggle at the idea, Adam came to her rescue.

'Sounds a mad scheme to me, Uno. What's the plan?'

Uno opened his waistcoat and disclosed a cummerbund round his waist. He unravelled it and to their surprise produced a long, thin strip of cloth at least twelve metres in length.

'Very strong,' he said, testing it with his paws. 'Take Miss Belle's weight.'

'But how does she get from one window to the next?' asked Candice.

'Tie end of cummerbund to dog's collar, hold other end. Throw dog out of this window, across space, in through passage window. Call dog. Dog enters through trapdoor. Secure end of cummerbund, thus have rope across space, strong enough support body. Body not need move, we pull through.'

Having heard the precise and gruesome details, Belle was struck dumb with apprehension and it was left to Adam to try and defend her against the general feeling that the plan might work and was, in fact, the only possible solution to the problem of how to escape from the chamber. Even her brother considered that she should agree to it. Candice was, to everyone's surprise, much in favour of the idea, provided that it was she and no one else who threw her pet across the chasm. Custard yelped with delight and seemed eager to do his bit. Eventually Damon said that, since they all had an interest in the successful result of the scheme, they ought to vote on it. He and Candice voted in favour, Adam against, Uno (since it was his idea) abstained, and they all looked at Belle. To everyone's amazement and relief, she said, after a brief hesitation – 'I'll do it on one condition. Otherwise, no way.'

'Name it,' said her brother.

'That I have some kind of a lifeline round me, just in case I fall.'

This was not only approved, but applauded as a suggestion as sensible as it was brilliant.

'Motion carried,' remarked Damon. 'Good girl, Belle, I'm proud of you.'

'Why did you change your mind?' Adam asked her, clearly unhappy at her decision.

She thought a moment, then said, 'Because at long last I feel I can do something you lot can't. I'm frightened – very much so – but at last I'm needed and it feels good. But one thing – you must all promise not to peek at me when I'm … I'm doing it.'

'Someone ought to watch you as you cross between

the windows,' objected Adam, then blushed as several pairs of eyes turned on him.

'Well, I don't mind Uno doing that,' said Belle.

Candice said impatiently, 'You needn't worry, Belle, no one will want to peek at you – it'd be different if it was me! But let's not worry about trivialities. We've sorted out all the important details, except one – WHEN do we do it?'

'I say sooner the better,' declared Damon.

'What, in broad daylight?' protested Adam. 'We'd never get past the guards. Surely we ought to wait until nightfall?'

'That's the way I felt about it at first,' said Damon. 'But, thinking it over, I can find at least three good reasons for going now. One: Sis oughtn't to have to make that trip across from window to window in darkness. Two: this lamp of mine isn't bright enough for us to find our way, and if we use flaming torches we'd be spotted in a flash. Three: they may come for us at any moment and then the fat would really be in the fire.'

'That's good enough for me,' asserted Candice, who was obviously agog for action and apparently ready to back Damon in everything.

Belle said, 'I agree with Damon. If I HAVE to cross that gap between the windows, I don't want to do it in the dark.'

'Uno?'

'No plan ideal. On balance, agree go now.'

The end of the cummerbund was tied securely to Custard's collar, whilst Candice held her pet in her arms and talked to it soothingly. It seemed as if the dog knew that something unwelcome was about to happen to him, because he was quiet and trembly and

194

nestled in her arms as though wanting to stay there. Tears came to the blonde girl's eyes as she coaxed the animal with loving reassurance, and eventually Damon said she ought to hurry as the longer the project was delayed the more dangerous it would become. So she stood at the window-slit, held the quivering animal securely in her grasp, said a quick prayer and hurled it across the chasm. The others, watching with their hearts in their mouths, saw the small black-and-white body hurtle across the void and disappear in through the window of the passage. They raised a quiet cheer, but Candice dashed to the door of their cell, crouched down at the open trapdoor and called, 'Custard! Here, Custard! Good dog then!' Within seconds the little dog scampered in through the trapdoor and yelped ecstatically, licking her face and whimpering with pleasure as she fussed over him. A few tears fell as she did so, and everyone else pretended not to notice.

Meanwhile, the two ends of the cummerbund were tied securely together and everyone hauled on it with all their strength to make certain that the circle of cloth moved freely. Then Damon turned to his sister.

'Up to you now, Belle,' he said gently. 'Ready?'

She gave a great gulp and nodded, unable to speak.

'Everybody turn their backs and pass me their belts,' said Damon. Whilst Belle undressed and placed her clothes by the small trapdoor, a lifeline was made by securing all the belts together. Then Belle said that she was ready and Uno took the lifeline and secured one end of it round her slim waist and tied the other end of it round his middle. Belle climbed up to the window-slit and slowly pressed her naked body into the narrow aperture.

'Not look down pliss?' suggested Uno calmly. 'Take time.'

Belle nodded and tried to squeeze through.

'I'm ... I'm not s-sure I can m-make it,' she gasped, wriggling frantically.

'You make it,' nodded Uno with confidence. 'Keep going.'

For a minute or two she struggled, gasping and crying out as the rough stonework grazed her flesh; then one almighty push did the trick and she was through, clinging to the edges of the window. Slowly, not daring to glance downwards into the shadowy depths below her, she lowered herself and clutched hold of the stretched cummerbund. Suddenly she was swinging from it, her legs dangling down into the dark abyss. The cummerbund sagged alarmingly and she could not repress a terrified squeal, but Uno tugged reassuringly on the lifeline and told her she was safe. He kept on talking to her as the others hauled on the cummerbund and she was drawn slowly across to the other side in a series of jerks that did nothing to ease her jangled nerves. Reaching the far wall, she swung her legs into the window-slit and worked her body through it, surprised and happy that it seemed slightly larger than the first one. Dropping to the stone floor of the passage, she released the lifeline, which was pulled back into the turret room. In the meantime, she ran through to the landing and Adam pushed her clothes through the trapdoor. But Damon hissed, 'Don't waste time dressing. Get those bolts open first!'

She drew the lower bolt back quite easily, despite its squeak of protest. But when she stretched up to the higher one and tried it, it refused to budge. She began

196

to wrestle with it, but stopped in sheer panic as she heard the clump, clump, clump of heavy boots on the stairs leading up to the landing.

'Oh!' she gasped, petrified with sudden fear. 'Help! Help! S-someone's coming!'

'Hurry up and draw the bolt then!' shouted Damon. 'Once we get out we can deal with him.'

Belle struggled desperately with the rusty metal, utter panic making her mouth dry, her body shiver and her hands act as if they were all thumbs. Crying with frustration, she battled with the refractory bolt, whilst the clump of the boots drew nearer and nearer. Then she screamed as a man in armour appeared at the top of the stairs, his visor up to disclose a thin, hard face with sharp eyes. He stopped dead on seeing her and for a moment stood motionless, clearly struck dumb with incomprehension, yet his piggy eyes gleaming at the sight of her unclothed girlish body.

In sheer panic she made one more tremendous effort and wrenched the bolt back in its socket. The guard uttered a guttural grunt and lumbered forward, drawing his curved scimitar. The door burst open, Belle staggered back behind it, the scimitar dug into the timber of the door with a thud, and Damon shot out of the turret room and dived for the guard's legs. He hugged them tightly, just as Adam and Candice erupted from the cell and hurled themselves at the tottering figure in armour. He was big and heavy, but Damon held his legs in a vice-like grip and he was unable to keep his balance. He swayed and grunted and suddenly collapsed and fell down onto his back with a resounding crash. It seemed to stun him, because he lay without making any effort to rise, although he kept on uttering weird grunting and clicking noises, and twitching all over, as though he could not help it.

'Reckon we should put him out of his misery?' suggested Candice, drawing her finger across her throat graphically.

'No!' exclaimed Adam. 'I say we don't. Look, let's not be bloodthirsty. He looks as though he's almost unconscious now. Let's just tie him up and shut him up in the cell. He won't trouble us any more.'

'I was NOT being bloodthirsty!' retorted Candice. 'But this is war, not a game. If they catch us escaping, they'll probably kill us, so why shouldn't we treat them the same?'

'Not unless we have to,' answered Adam. 'The fact that they are barbarous savages – and I'm not yet certain that they ARE – is no reason for us to behave in the same way.'

'Not make sense,' reproved Uno. Adam glanced at him angrily, ready to argue further, when Uno took the wind out of his sails by adding, 'But agree. Use cummerbund, pliss.'

Whilst they bound and gagged the guard and dragged him into the turret room, Damon appropriated the man's weapon and Belle hastily dressed. They bolted the door and Candice tucked Custard under her arm. The little group, having entered the cell four in number, and exited it as five, stood on the landing, looking down the flight of wooden steps to the dark regions below.

'Well, this is where we sally forth,' announced Damon cheerfully. 'Hi-ho for the jolly old dungeons and the glorious Chalice.'

'And the Guardian,' Adam reminded him pessimistically. 'And the Black Baron. And the soldiers. And all

198

kinds of unknown obstacles and dangers that lie in front of us.'

'Don't be so gloomy,' said Damon with a laugh. 'Nothing ventured, nothing gained – isn't that what they say? And there ARE five of us. The Famous Five ... the Invincible Five ... the Victorious Five. All for one and one for all. This is an historic moment.'

'Yes, well, don't let it go to your head,' advised Candice, stroking Custard's head as he looked up at her with trusting eyes. 'To give YOU a quotation for a change – there's many a slip 'twixt cup and lip. I'm with you all the way but, in a situation like this, to give you yet one more quotation – softly softly catchee monkey.'

'No monkeys here,' said Uno.

'I haven't come all this way to catch stupid monkeys,' asserted Damon.

'I know what you mean, Candice,' said Belle, looking wise. 'You mean look before you leap.'

Adam groaned. 'I say let's have done with the quotations, shall we?'

'Too much talk,' said Uno severely. 'We go now.'

4

They crept very quietly down the steep wooden steps, holding their breath, and wincing at each creak and crack of the old timbers. At the bottom they huddled, listening. When no sounds came to their ears, they moved along the passage on tiptoe, hearts beating faster than usual, every sense alert for possible danger. Damon had taken the lead, mainly because the others assumed he had some knowledge of the way down to the dungeons, although it was a fact that he tended to be in the forefront of any enterprise in which he took part. Uno was the oldest among them, but he was very small and at the same time he appeared to have no wish to be in the vanguard. Candice followed Damon, still holding her dog tightly; Uno was in the middle; and Belle followed him, with Adam bringing up the rear. When a couple of dark doorways showed up, Damon halted and the others grouped round him.

'What's the hold-up?' asked Adam in a low voice.

'Just checking that we're on the right track,' replied Damon, a shade too casually.

'What you're saying is you don't know WHERE we are!' said Candice tartly.

'I know where we are,' he replied. 'Well, at least I've got a fair idea. Don't worry, everything's under control. Follow your Uncle Damon and you'll be alright, believe me.'

He set off again down the corridor at a spanking pace and the others had to hurry to keep up with him. They went down another flight of steps – stone ones this time – and were traversing yet another corridor when the sound of a number of heavy clumping boots hitting the flagstoned floor in unison smote their ears.

'It's a patrol!' exclaimed Damon. 'Quick, in here!'

They happened to be passing a door at the time. It was shut, but Damon opened it, and within seconds they were all inside the chamber, huddled behind the closed door and listening with baited breath as the clumsy clump, clump, clump of boots rang along the corridor and the owners thereof marched past. They waited until the sounds of the crunching boots had entirely died away, and then they all heaved a sigh of relief.

'A miss is as good as a mile,' remarked Belle, who (as Adam had by now realised) could always be relied upon for an appropriate and pithy motto to suit the occasion.

'I reckon it's all clear,' nodded Damon. 'We'd better…'

He stopped as Candice took hold of his arm. 'Have you seen what's behind us?' she hissed.

This was enough to cause all of them to turn swiftly. There followed a concerted gasp. The chamber was large, and furnished as a bedroom – in fact, as a lady's boudoir. In the centre stood a double-sized four-poster bed, hung with rich draperies. In the bed lay a girl, aged perhaps seventeen, possibly eighteen. She was extremely well-favoured, with a smooth, white skin of a texture akin to that of fine porcelain china, a perfectly-shaped nose, red lips, and a mass of black hair, long and smooth and shiny as a raven's wing, resting on the soft lace-edged pillow. Her figure, discernible under the luxurious bedclothes, was exquisite. Her bosom rose and fell evenly.

'The sleeping beauty!' whispered Belle, almost with awe.

'Just what I was thinking,' nodded Damon, who was quite obviously feasting his eyes on the lovely vision.

'But why here, in this room, in this castle?' asked Adam in a bewildered voice.

'Why not?' argued Damon. 'Why not here just as much as anywhere else? She's clearly of very high rank, so she could be the Black Baron's daughter, although since she's so beautiful I rather doubt that. And she IS beautiful, isn't she? I don't think I've ever seen anyone so perfect of face and figure.'

'She's alright,' said Candice begrudgingly, putting Custard down onto the floor but keeping a tight hold on his cord. 'I can't say I go for that fragile ethereal type of good looks myself – they tend to go off quite quickly, and grow fat and plain and lose all their beauty. Besides, what good would they be outside the bedroom? Put them in a situation where there's a spot of danger and they'd scream with horror and faint off. Useless.'

'Poppycock!' said Damon rudely. 'You're just jealous.'

Candice made a noise that was coarsely expressive. 'Jealous? Of her? Huh! I'd like to see her wrestle a bear, as I did; or run the hind legs off a deer, as I did; or leap across a wide canal as I did – only yesterday, IF you recall.'

'Yes, but we're talking about beauty, not physical prowess,' replied Damon scornfully. 'There are other things in life besides athletics, you know. What do you think of her, Uno?'

202

'Lady pretty. But not sleeping beauty.'

'Well, I disagree,' stated Damon firmly. 'And I'm going to try to wake her up. She looks good and kind, and if I can wake her up I'm sure she'll want to help us.'

'Not sleeping beauty,' repeated Uno.

Ignoring the little dwarf, and before anyone could stop him, Damon had approached the bed and bent over the serene and sweet face of the sleeping girl.

'Recommend not touch!' warned Uno. 'Not good. Believe...'

Damon bent lower and planted a kiss on the red lips – then staggered back in shocked horror as the slender girl-like figure reared up from the bed in a trice. The onlookers too watched with petrified fear as the girl's body writhed and squirmed and then swiftly metamorphosed into the sleek shining shape of a huge black panther that crouched on the bed and glared at them with small red eyes burning with feral hatred, and snarled at them with jaws gaping wide to show a red slavering mouth and rows of razor-sharp teeth. Custard gave it one horrified look, then yelped feebly and backed behind Candice's feet.

Damon recovered his wits very quickly and, drawing from his belt the scimitar he had taken from the guard on the landing, swung at the panther. But the animal reacted with lightning speed and lashed out with a giant forepaw, knocking the weapon clean out of Damon's grasp and leaving his arm numb and him defenceless. The onlookers seemed to be affected with a strange inertia and were unable to move a muscle to assist their comrade. The panther crouched lower, snarled with incredible ferocity and was clearly on the point of springing at Damon. But Uno shook himself free of the paralysis that had gripped the watchers, flung up a handful of white powder and muttered aloud a series of weird, unintelligible sounds. The effect was dramatic. The panther had already started its spring as Uno threw up the powder and its body was in mid-air when it dissolved instantly into nothingness, disappearing to leave no trace whatsoever of its presence. Everyone stared in blank amazement, Damon in particular gazing first at the empty space where the panther had been, and then at Uno with a mixture of bewilderment and awe. Candice was the first to find a voice.

'That'll teach you to think twice before you start kissing girls, Damon,' she said tartly. Then to Uno, with respect, 'You knew it was a phantom?'

'Not know. Suspected,' replied Uno serenely. 'Lucky I right.'

'Lucky indeed,' said Adam with great sincerity, expelling his breath with a noisy exhalation.

'Oh Uno, how marvellous of you!' exclaimed Belle, and she embraced the little furry dwarf, to the latter's manifest embarrassment.

Damon spoke to him, in a tone bordering on the reverential.

'Mind telling me how you did that?' he enquired. 'It could come in VERY handy indeed in my profession.'

Candice spoke to him in tones indicating that his recent behaviour had considerably diminished her good opinion of him. 'I would have thought that people in YOUR "profession" – as you term it – wouldn't go around taking stupid and unnecessary risks like kissing girls that turn into panthers.'

'Life without risk is like a meal without wine,' replied

Damon blithely, thus augmenting the family reputation for proverbs. 'For instance, I'd be quite prepared this very moment to do the same to you, just to see what you'd turn into.'

'I was out walking along a lane one day,' remarked Adam casually. 'And I turned into a field.'

To his chagrin, everyone ignored him and Uno said, 'Too much talk. We go on.'

Candice picked up the dog and they quitted the chamber, which they observed had now lost all its feminine trappings and had reverted to a bare room with stone walls and a curtainless window looking out onto another wall. They headed off down the corridor in the opposite direction to that taken by the marching feet. They came to a T-junction, new corridors leading left and right and both disappearing round dark bends.

'Well, mastermind, which way?' Candice asked Damon with malicious relish.

He grinned cheerfully. 'Goodness knows. Shall we toss a coin?'

'You don't know, do you!' said Candice. 'You have the gall to take the lead and you bring us all this way, and now you don't know which direction to take. You're ... you're nothing but a fraud!'

'True, but a good-looking one,' Damon replied serenely.

'Oh, you're hopeless!' She punched him on the arm, but the blow had no real force behind it and Adam suspected that it was more affectionate than anything else.

'Let's vote on it,' suggested Adam. 'I say left.'

'And I say...' began Candice, ready to start an

argument, but she stopped when Belle hissed 'Sssh!' and held up a warning forefinger.

'What...?' began Adam, but she shook her head wordlessly and laid a finger against his mouth. They remained quiet after that, standing in a silent and motionless group, cocking their heads to catch the slightest sound.

'Yes,' nodded Candice. 'I can hear something now.'

'Me also,' added Uno.

'And me,' said Damon. 'But what is it?'

'I can tell you,' declared Belle. 'Someone is being badly beaten. I can hear the sound of repeated blows, and moans and shrieks. It's coming from the passage to the right.'

'Well, we can't have that,' said Adam decidedly. 'Let's go.'

'Are you absolutely sure we should interfere?' objected Damon. 'Remember we are here for a purpose – and not to interfere in matters that don't concern us. Besides, do we really want to reveal our presence here?'

'Yes I know, but we can't just stand by and not do anything about it!' ejaculated Adam. 'Sounds as though the victim is taking terrible punishment.'

'I agree with Adam,' said Belle at once.

'Well I don't,' said Candice flatly. 'If we want to do what we came here to do, AND get out alive, it'd be madness to get sidetracked just because of something that's probably happening every day of the week in this diabolical place.'

'What do you say, Uno?' Adam asked him, hoping the little dwarf would take his side in the argument.

'Maybe another trick.'

'Trick?' repeated Adam.

206

'Like lady into panther,' Uno explained patiently.

'How could it be a trick?' Adam demanded.

'Yes, I see what you mean, Uno,' said Belle slowly. 'It could be. It sounds as though it's coming from all around us, and that can't be right. I don't like it, Adam. Once bitten, twice shy.'

There was a pause and, in the ensuing silence, they heard the sounds clearly, the dreadful lash, lash, lash of fierce blow upon fierce blow, the gurgling screams and fearful moans of the victim intermingling.

'Listen to it!' exclaimed Adam. 'How CAN we stand by and let that go on happening? If the rest of you want to stay here, do so: I'm going on.' And with that he sped off down the passage to the right.

'Impulsive lad,' commented Damon impassively. 'I suppose we'd better go as well. Keep your famous powder ready, Uno.'

'Not much left,' answered Uno as they followed Adam down the passage. They rounded a bend and bumped into their quarry as he stood outside a door, listening intently.

'I think it's this one,' he said doubtfully.

'Well, open it up, slowcoach, and let's see,' suggested Candice, still showing signs of impatience.

Adam turned the handle and threw the door open wide. They gazed into another room. This one also contained a bed, as did the previous chamber, but whereas the other was, on first sight at least, luxurious, ornate and very feminine, this one was small, dark and sparsely-furnished. The bed, which was against the stone wall, was small and narrow, the bedclothes thin, tattered and grimy. Under the bedclothes huddled an old man. He had a straggly white beard and his face was lined and hollow-cheeked; his eyes were filmed over and sunk deep into dark sockets, his mouth was thin-lipped and trembling weakly. His body appeared to be badly emaciated and the hands that gripped the sheets were bony and feeble. As they entered the room, he turned his head slowly on the grubby pillow, looked at them and murmured, in a weak, piping voice, 'Welcome.'

They stared around the room, but there were no other doors, and the stone walls appeared to be solid. The old man looked as though he hadn't moved for many hours. There was absolutely no sign of anyone having been involved in a beating session.

'Those sounds have stopped,' said Belle. They listened, and realised that she had spoken the truth.

Damon spoke to the old man. 'We heard someone receiving a beating – and a bad one. It doesn't look as though it was in here. Do you know anything about it?'

The old man managed to find enough strength to raise his bushy eyebrows, and piped, 'Hey? A beating, did you say?' He frowned, as though finding the words difficult to understand, and fractionally raised his head. 'What sort of beating?'

'We all heard it,' said Adam in perplexity. 'The sounds of someone getting an awful lot of punishment: lots of blows, and the victim screaming and moaning...'

'Oh THAT!' The old man's head fell wearily back onto his pillow. 'Don't you worry your young heads about that. It comes and goes, comes and goes. Mostly at night, I reckon. Yes, mostly at night.'

'But where does it come from?' asked Belle, bewildered.

'Hey? Did you say where?' Again he raised his head slightly and attempted a feeble cackle. 'You mean ... when ... don't you, not "where".'

'When?' repeated Belle, now thoroughly mystified, as were her companions.

'You should be asking "when's it coming from"!' he cackled.

'"When's it coming from"?' repeated Damon. 'He's a few stars short of a constellation!'

'Oh no I ain't,' said the old man. ''Cause the answer is ... a long time ago. In fact, a VERY long time ago. Before you was born, that's for sure. I started young in the trade, d'ye see; full of enthusiasm, I was. But then I wanted to make it my career. I was that young and foolish.' He replaced his head on the pillow. 'Wasn't at it very long, though, not ALL that many years. Sickened, I was. Sickened by it all. No one told me about that, they didn't. No one told me about being so sickened that I couldn't eat, couldn't sleep. So I packed it in. Couldn't stand it no more, could I? Gave it up, all them long years ago. But, trouble is, it won't give me up, d'ye see? Comes back now and then. Keeps on coming back. Don't matter where I am, what I'm doing. And, now I'm old, I don't do much any more, and what with that, and me being frail, well, it comes back more and more. At night, mostly, so's I can't sleep. Mostly at night.' He lay still and quiet for a minute, then slowly raised his head and his lined face grimaced. 'Here it comes again. Won't leave me alone. Won't ever leave me alone.'

The others could hear it as well now, the distant but distinct sounds of a vicious and violent beating; the heavy, sadistic blows, one after the other, on and on and on; and the hideous moans and screams, and the pitiful whimpering in between. Whilst the old man lay wearily, cringing under the cumulative horror, sick at heart, his audience stared at one another in bewilderment.

'What does he mean?' Belle asked, perplexed and scared.

'Understand,' nodded Uno. He spoke to the old man. 'You in charge dungeons long ago, beat many prisoners, maybe kill some. Your duty – maybe not like, but do it. Now retired, but echoes of past return haunt you. Suffer now as victims suffered in past.'

'Most nights,' said the old man tiredly. 'Sometimes all night long. You don't know – you can't know – how bad it can be. I . . . I can't take much more. Haunted, all because of my past mistakes . . . haunted . . .'

'Not hauntings,' said Uno. 'Not in true sense. Creation of own guilty conscience. Mind, racked by remorse, makes monkey on back, punishment for past sins, self-castigation.'

The old man stared at him with dull eyes.

'You trying to make out them noises ain't real? I can hear them all the time, all the time. They're real alright.'

'WE hear them,' said Uno. 'But not real. Fabrication of mind tortured by desire-atonement very strong, everyone hear. Maybe strong enough see. But not real.'

Whilst the old man continued to stare at him in disbelief, Damon said, 'I get it, Uno! And your powder can get rid of it, just like the panther?'

'No. Powder for creations sorcery. This product disordered brain. Needs different treatment.' He looked at the invalid: due to his small stature, his eyes were level with the old man's face. 'Permit me help you.'

He laid his furry paws on the aged head, looked

210

deep into the rheumy eyes and began to intone syllables that Adam thought sounded like a chant of some kind, but with words he couldn't catch and in a sort of music he'd never heard before. After about five minutes of this, Uno talked to his patient in an undertone, whilst the others watched and waited, eager to see if Uno succeeded in his endeavours but at the same time impatient to be on their way.

Suddenly, just as though someone had switched them off, the noises stopped. The old man's eyes were at first suspicious, then puzzled. He raised his head, slowly, questioningly.

'They're ... they're gone,' he quavered. 'But mark my words they'll be back.'

'No,' said Uno.

They waited, but the noises didn't return. The old man looked at Uno, then at the others.' 'You hear them, maybe?'

They assured him they didn't. He continued to stare incredulously at them, but eventually tears came into his eyes and he clasped Uno's paws with such heartfelt relief and gratitude that it was pitiful to behold. Uno talked to him for another few minutes and soon the old man lay back in his bed, resting quietly, a look of such happiness on his face that it erased half the wrinkles in his leathery skin.

Damon said they should be on their way, and told the old man where they were headed and why. The ancient gripped his hand.

'Good luck to you,' he whispered. 'You'll need it. I've never seen the Guardian, but I've heard it – and I've heard many terrible tales about it. I'd like to help you, but I've very little money...'

211

'We wouldn't take your money, old man,' said Candice gently.

'Wouldn't do you no good, anyway. But I DO want to reward you.' The old man raised his head again and looked around him, then pointed to a bag hanging on one of the bedposts. 'Look inside that. You'll find a parchment. Take it, it's yours. And when you are in dire need, read it – it may be of help to you.'

As though his talking had exhausted him, he lay back and closed his eyes. Adam ferreted inside the threadbare bag and extracted from it a small sheet of yellow parchment with a red ribbon tied round it. It felt odd, and seemed to move in his fingers, almost as though it were *alive*; a vague vapour appeared to drift up from it. He looked at the old man. 'Thanks,' he said.

The old man opened his eyes. 'You're welcome,' he said drowsily. Then, with a slight smile, 'They're still gone, you know.'

'They not return,' said Uno confidently.

The old man nodded and closed his eyes again. They tiptoed out of the room and closed the door. As they walked down the passage, Candice was obviously consumed with curiosity and said to Adam, 'What's on the parchment?'

'Hold on a moment,' interposed Damon. He looked at Uno. 'What did you do and say to the old codger to cure him?'

'Old man halfway to cure when learned truth about affliction,' said Uno. 'Then used self-knowledge, self-help, plus secret techniques belong our race. Regret cannot reveal. You humans one fault: misuse knowledge for evil, not good.'

'I wouldn't quarrel with you about that,' said Damon ruefully.

'Adam, what's on the parchment?' asked Belle. 'I'm as curious as Candice to know.'

'You girls!' he said tolerantly. Then, to Belle, 'Don't you know the old saying "Curiosity killed the cat"?'

'I'm not a cat,' replied Belle indignantly. 'But I've got one back home. I call her Snowball because she's all white.'

'Better than being all wong,' said Adam with a straight face.

'Read the parchment!' said Candice impatiently.

Adam untied the ribbon and unfolded the parchment. He read the words on it, then grimaced. 'Some kind of riddle, I suppose. Listen:

'When the dreamer awakes
Then dies his dream
When the pale moon sets
Then fades its beam
So muffle the church bells
No more will they chime
And kill off the poet
No more will he rhyme.'

'Is that all?' asked Belle, disappointed.

Adam nodded, refurled the parchment and retied the ribbon round it.

'What's it mean?' asked Damon. 'Sounds like a load of nonsense to me. Any ideas, Uno?'

'No. Ponder same as we go. Not waste time.'

'Time and tide wait for no man,' quoted Belle.

They went on their way.

5

They negotiated another flight of stone steps leading downwards without encountering any opposition, and their hopes began to rise as Damon gave it as his opinion that they were now nearing the ground floor. Despite the fact that it was daylight outside, the interior of the Castle was exceedingly gloomy and this proved to be a distinct advantage. At the foot of the flight of steps there were three corridors all leading off, and a short debate took place as to which one they should take. Eventually it was decided to adopt the middle course and once more they set out, treading quietly and with great caution over the ancient flagstones.

About halfway along, Belle hissed, 'Hush! I can hear something.' At once they halted, as if by now they had realised that her sense of hearing was far more acute than theirs and warranted respectful attention. But as soon as they stood silently, they all heard the same sound.

'People,' said Damon succinctly. 'A sizeable gathering, I would judge. I reckon we're getting near to the Great Hall of the Castle and it could be about lunchtime!'

'Well, we COULD go back, I suppose,' said Adam reluctantly. 'But it means back to the stairway; we've not passed any doors or passages along this corridor.'

'I don't like retreating,' said Damon obstinately.

'There were two other corridors back there,' Candice reminded him. 'Either one might be better than...'

Another sound reached their ears. This one was much louder, and much more ominous in that it came from the direction of the stairway they had recently descended, and consisted of a noise with which they were becoming familiar – the distant but approaching clump, clump, clump of heavy boots on the stone floor.

'Great bellowing bullfrogs!' exclaimed Candice. 'It's another of those infernal patrols, and headed this way. Now we're in the soup.'

'Maybe not,' answered Uno. 'Depends what at other end passage.'

Even as he spoke, soldiers in armour appeared by the foot of the stairs, turning into their corridor. As the group of five stared in mesmerised horror, they saw a patrol of nine men, with one in front leading the remainder. In an instant the fugitives were spotted, hoarse cries came from the patrol, scimitars were drawn and the nine armoured soldiers lurched towards them.

With one accord the escaped prisoners wheeled about and raced along the corridor away from their pursuers. They were encouraged by the fact that they were able to move much faster than those behind them, and the distance between them rapidly increased. As they neared the end of the corridor they saw that it ended in an archway, and opened out onto a sort of gallery protected by a wooden balustrade overlooking an area below. The noise of a large crowd grew louder, and they were able to distinguish chatter (mostly in deep voices), much shouting, laughter (mainly masculine guffaws), the clatter of implements and crockery, background music from stringed instruments, and the barking of numerous dogs (which made Candice put her hand over Custard's mouth),

215

Reaching the archway, they emerged onto the gallery and saw that it did indeed overlook a large hall. The gallery ran all the way round the hall, about ten metres above the flagstoned floor, culminating in two flights of stairs leading down to where a banquet was in progress. They had time only to note that some thirty or so people – mostly men – were seated at an enormously long wooden table piled with dishes of food, together with numerous carafes of wine, tankards, bowls of fruit, boxes of sweetmeats and other adjuncts to such a meal. A number of female attendants bustled around serving the diners and, in one corner, three musicians plucked at their instruments, producing a plaintive melody that was almost drowned by the general hubbub. All round the periphery of the hall, under arches supporting the gallery, were more soldiers in armour, standing stiffly to attention, scimitars at the ready.

'Trapped!' said Candice tersely.

'Oh goodness!' whispered Belle. 'What do we do now?'

'Rule of battle,' said Uno placidly. 'When caught between forces, attack weaker one.'

'You mean the patrol coming up behind us,' said Damon, and they turned to confront the eight armoured soldiers and their leader who were now only a few metres away. Adam noticed that, whilst the leader had his visor up displaying his angry red face, and ran with a reasonable degree of freedom of movement, his henchmen had their visors in place, hiding their faces, and they lumbered along in a jerky mechanical fashion, rather like...

'Robots!' he yelled, and dived to the floor to stretch full-length at the leader's boots. Unable to stop in time, the man tripped over him and fell at the base of the balustrade, Adam's companions scattering to give him room. The eight armoured minions came blundering along, waving their scimitars with jerky menace, and one by one they tripped over the leader's recumbent body. The two in the vanguard of the patrol lurched forward heavily against the balustrade, which fractured with a loud splintering and rending of timber, causing them to fall over the edge down into the hall below. The remainder, pressing blindly on behind, fared in exactly the same way, stumbling through the wide gap and plunging some ten metres down to the flagstones below. The eightfold impact was accompanied by a horrendous din of crashing platemail and clanging metal; when the adventurers looked over the rail they saw nothing but a scattered heap of metal parts, fragments of armour, and other assorted bits and pieces, none of which looked remotely human.

'By the Great Ruler in the Sky, Adam, you were right!' breathed Damon.

The leader, who was manifestly not a robot, tried to rise, but his heavy armour hampered him. Whilst Adam scrambled away, the others seized the struggling figure, lifted him up, rushed him to the edge of the gallery and tipped him over. He fell with a roar that turned into a grunting gasp as he hit the pile of sundered armour with a tremendous cacophony of crashing metal. He twitched violently, then lay unmoving.

'Great stuff, Adam!' Damon congratulated him breathlessly. 'You realised they were robots long before I did.'

'Very good,' nodded Uno, and Adam glowed with pride.

'That's all very well,' said practical Candice, bringing them all back down to earth. 'But the fat's truly in the fire now. They've seen us.'

The huge hall below was now a scene of frenetic activity, as though it were a giant ants' nest that had just been disturbed. Men who had been seated at the table a moment before were scrambling up from their places and shouting orders at one another; serving wenches were rushing about, dropping trays and platters and squealing in utter panic; the figures in armour round the hall were moving jerkily and not in unison, forming and reforming into various military groupings and shuffling together with much clattering of metal on metal; the musicians were obviously scared out of their wits and were playing hopelessly out of tune and at different tempos; and there was an overall impression of total chaos. To add to the din, Custard was yelping excitedly from the harbour of Candice's arms.

Damon pointed. One party of armoured figures, led by a man not in armour and brandishing a long sword, was climbing the stairs at the far end, their eyes fixed on the small group in the gallery.

'No good facing that lot,' he said decidedly. 'We'd better head back where we came from and take one of those other two passages leading off from the foot of the stairs.'

Accordingly he led them along the corridor away from the Great Hall, traversing the full length of it to reach the stairs and the other two passages. As they reached the intersection, soldiers appeared at the far end of the passage to the left, so all five fugitives ran in the opposite direction. At the end of the passage a further flight of stairs came into view, leading down.

'This looks promising!' exclaimed Damon, and dived through an archway and down the stairs. It was in the form of a tight spiral and their rate of descent was so great that they grew quite dizzy as they rushed round and round, heading downwards all the time. The stairs decanted them one by one into a dark hall, lit only by diffused illumination filtering in through vertical slits in the walls high above their heads. The lower part of the chamber was almost in darkness and they peered about them, trying to pierce the gloom with their eyes. Unfortunately, Damon had dropped his lamp during the scuffle in the gallery, so that they did not even have the benefit of whatever light it would have provided.

'Bless me, it IS dark down here,' murmured Belle uneasily. 'I don't seem to be able to see any way out. Can anyone else...' She stopped and her mouth opened wide in a shrill scream. A trembling finger pointed ahead. 'There's ... there's something horrible – there!'

Everyone drew together nervously and stared in the direction indicated by her quivering finger. The hair at the back of Adam's neck prickled as he saw what appeared to be a bunch of enormously tall creatures with pipe-cleaner legs, long, thin arms and huge, bloated white heads. They seemed to waver, as though seen through moving water. The five companions huddled closer for protection, and the clump of menacing unknowns tightened their grouping in a similar manner.

'I don't want to worry you, but you'll see others to our left,' murmured Candice in an undertone. The others turned and saw another congregation of creatures. These were fat, repulsive-looking specimens, with squat enormously-swollen bodies, grotesque balloon-like legs, and, in absurd contrast, very small heads. Custard saw them, whined feebly and tried to burrow further into the protection afforded by Candice's arms.

'What have we got ourselves into?' asked Damon in a hushed voice, clearly shaken by the outlandish appearance of the newcomers. 'And why don't they move, or say something?'

'There's another lot,' whispered Adam, pointing in a third direction. This collection was even more deformed, possessing chunky torsos connected to giant hips and massive legs by means of virtually non-existent middles. They did not appear to have any heads, but their arms were so long they reached to the floor and at the ends of each there were enormous hands. This group stood like the others, bunched closely together and, as far as could be determined in the case of creatures without heads, facing them.

The five companions in the centre of the darkened room moved slightly as they watched the strange assortment of creatures, and the creatures behaved in a similar fashion, as though trying to imitate them.

'There seems to be about the same number in each group,' whispered Damon. 'I wonder if it's some sort of contest. I wish we had more light. I think we ought to make a move before those soldiers catch up with us.'

He took a few tentative steps towards the group of very fat creatures, and was startled to see one of them move towards him as though to meet him. Adam went forward to join him, and a second bloated creature detached itself from its fellows and joined the first.

'Perhaps they want a pow-wow?' suggested Adam in an undertone.

'I don't know,' admitted Damon. 'But I'm getting tired of this.' Suddenly he threw caution to the winds. 'All right then!' he shouted, drawing his scimitar. 'Enough of this dilly-dallying! Let's see what you're made of!'

Ignoring the fact that his antagonist was also waving a strange-looking weapon in the air, Damon dashed forward towards his foe.

Bang!

He reeled back, dropped his scimitar and fell over, dazed. The onlookers behind him were amazed to see Damon's opponent do exactly the same thing. Adam took a hurried step backwards. HIS antagonist did precisely the same thing. There was a brief hiatus, then Uno spoke.

'Understand. No one here but us. Distorting mirrors.'

'What?' gasped Belle.

'I was beginning to suspect that myself,' nodded Candice.

Adam went forward and helped Damon to his feet, whilst the rest of them investigated the situation and found that Uno was right. They were standing in the centre of a number of high mirrors that distorted all reflections, each acting in a different manner.

'So we were really seeing ourselves!' giggled Belle.

'And Damon ran full-tilt into a mirror!' chuckled Candice. 'That'll teach him to run blindly into something without thinking it out first.'

'I didn't notice YOU coming up with the right answer,' snapped Damon, rubbing his bruised forehead and nose ruefully.

'Why should I?' she replied tartly. 'You're supposed to be the professional. I'm not your keeper, you know.'

'The job's on offer,' he said to her with a cheerful grin. 'Good pay – and prospects even better. Fancy it?'

She disdained to reply and Uno suggested that they should be going. Accordingly they searched for a way out, and soon discovered a door located behind one of the mirrors. Damon opened it and peered through.

'Seems all right,' he said quietly. 'There are some more stairs here, leading down. They may, with a bit of luck, go all the way to the dungeons. Follow your uncle Damon.'

They stepped through the doorway. Immediately the door closed behind them, and clicked shut. Candice, who was last through, uttered an exclamation and tried the door.

'Locked!' she said in dismay.

'That's bad,' said Damon. He looked at the locked door, then shrugged.

'Well, that settles it: we've no option but to go on.'

He began to descend the stairs and they followed him. They were about halfway down when, without any warning whatsoever, the stairs swivelled and turned so that they were level with one another to form a smooth and steeply-inclined slope. Thus bereft of any support, the five hapless adventurers – plus the dog – slid down the declivity on their backs, with many a gasp, moan, groan and gurgle, landing in a confused and commingled heap at the bottom.

When they had sorted themselves out, sat up and stared around, with Custard whining and wriggling in Candice's arms, they found that they were entirely surrounded by men in armour, scimitars drawn, and a leader who, with visor raised, grinned sardonically down at them.

The leader looked down at them with the sort of look he might have given to a sty-full of pigs. They saw, with dismay, that it was the same man who had been in charge of the escort to the Castle. He still had a red face and his expression, as he leered down at them, was – if anything – even more brutal than it had been earlier.

'Caught you, I reckon,' he said with great satisfaction. His brows drew together. 'You've led us a bit of a dance, you have, but it's all over now. You're properly caught, you are, and you won't escape so easily again, you can lay to that. Come on, on your feet now – the Master himself wants to have a chat with you.' He guffawed and they winced at the familiar sound. 'I reckon he's thinking up something REALLY tasty for your last hour on this earth, and because of that he wants to see what you look like. So come on, step lively now. Get on your feet and MOVE! And shut that animal up if you don't want me to shut him in my own way!'

The five picked themselves up and Candice hushed Custard up as best she could, smoothing his ruffled fur. Damon faced the leader boldly.

'You say we're going to see the Black Baron himself?' he asked.

'That's exactly what I said. Come on!'

Escorted by the armoured henchmen, with the leader in front, they were taken along passages and through an archway into the Great Hall itself. The many people thronging the huge chamber – the men and women seated at the long trestle-table that groaned under the weight of provender, the serving wenches that bustled around them, the guards in armour once more stiffly to attention, and the musicians (now joined by jugglers, clowns and acrobats) – were all back once again at their normal activities. The Hall, with its high-vaulted ceiling, its gallery around the upper part, and its colonnade around the lower part, thrummed once again with the babble of conversation, punctuated by guffaws and giggles, shouts and squeals, backed by the clatter of implements and crockery, by tinkling music and by the panting of the jugglers and acrobats as they performed their acts. The prisoners were taken the full length of the Hall, over the flagstoned floor, jeered at by the men at the table, stared at by the bold-faced serving wenches, mocked by the clowns and jugglers, and ignored by the guards (robot or otherwise).

As they were marched past the table, Damon nudged Adam.

'See the man in the green cloak, lots of grey hair and no beard? Next to the fat woman in pink?'

Adam nodded.

'That's the Lord of the Treasury. That's the man you want to see about your father.'

Adam turned his gaze eagerly on the man indicated by Damon. The Lord of the Treasury's face was stern, but not severe. He wore a distinct air of authority, but did not have the brutal appearance possessed by so many of his colleagues. Adam decided he might be amenable to persuasion and looked forward to talking with him.

'Silence!' roared one of the escorts, proving that he was no robot, and Damon received a violent push in the back that sent him staggering forward so that he stumbled and fell. Adam helped him to his feet, aware of raucous laughter and jeering from the watching crowds.

They were led to the head of the table, where sat an imposing personage on a high-backed throne that looked as though it was made from solid gold, intricately-worked. He was flanked on either side by comely women, one a brunette in a green robe, the other a blonde-haired female in a red robe. The personage himself was clad all in black – black jerkin, black breeches, black cloak, black gloves – and his beard too was jet black, as were his cruel gleaming eyes. His face was pale, with high cheekbones and a thin-lipped mouth with the corners turned downwards.

'These are the five criminals, Master,' said the leader in a cringing voice.

The Master carried on pulling apart a peach with his long, slender fingers, peeling off the skin and tearing at the exposed flesh with malicious relish. Finally he turned his head very slowly and coldly surveyed the five prisoners, running his black eyes over them one by one, from head to foot. Adam felt his spine tingle and his hair prickle as the hard eyes examined him as a scientist might have viewed a laboratory specimen ready for dissection. Then the Master spoke.

'I am the Black Baron of Xakkara,' he said. His voice was harsh and, although not loud, carried unmistakeable tones of arrogance and menace. 'You are here in my Castle with one aim – to abuse my hospitality by stealing my Chalice. For that crime you will all surely perish.'

'The quality of mercy is not strained,' said Belle informatively. 'It droppeth as the...'

'Silence!' snapped the Black Baron.

'I will NOT be silent!' retorted Belle indignantly. 'I shall...'

225

'Leave it, Sis,' counselled Damon. 'Let me handle it.'
He looked calmly at the Black Baron. 'Excuse me
contradicting you, but we did not come to steal YOUR
Chalice. I came here entirely off my own bat to remove
the Chalice from where you have hidden it and return
it to its rightful owners, the High Priests of Zaire. This
is my mission which, despite all you may say or do,
I shall yet accomplish. These others with me are people
who were thrown into my cell only yesterday. They
have nothing to do with me or my mission.'

'You lie!' said the Black Baron with cold scorn. 'You
are a stupid and foolish urchin. That ... that person...'
he indicated Belle, '...is your sister. Do you deny this?'

'No,' Damon shrugged. 'I had forgotten you were a
sorcerer.'

'You will do well NOT to forget it. Yet there is one
among you who is a servant of a man who, although
clearly my inferior, is something of a minor practitioner
of the black arts.' He stared arrogantly at Uno. 'I
presume you will not deny this?'

'No,' replied Uno serenely. 'Me proud to be number
one servant Master Castroglio – who not inferior to
you.'

'Good for you, Uno!' cried Adam.

'Silence!' The Black Baron kept his eyes on Uno. 'It
is as well that you have admitted it. How else could
you have the means of circumventing my little ruse of
the captive princess on the islet, and the sleeping beauty
here in the Castle? Your master has a minor talent, but
he can never aspire to match my skill and my knowledge,
which are unique.'

'Humans have saying,' said Uno impassively. 'Pride
goeth before a fall.'

226

'I was just going to say that!' ejaculated Belle indignantly.

'Silence!' The Black Baron's cold gaze turned on Adam, who felt a shiver travel up his spine. 'And now YOU, little boy. Why have YOU come here? Are you this urchin's accomplice or – as he so foolishly suggests – merely a chance acquaintance?'

'I came here with the intention of stealing the Chalice as well,' said Adam deliberately, vastly annoyed at being addressed as 'little boy'. 'And, since Damon here has prior claim, I'll do everything I can to help him.'

Adam's natural apprehension at his impulsive statement was slightly assuaged when he felt Belle press his hand admiringly.

'Silence!' The Black Baron now turned his eyes on Candice. 'As for you, I believe you came here to help the other criminals and therefore you are equally guilty and a criminal as well. Do you deny this?'

'What's the point?' said Candice disdainfully. 'You seem to know it all. The answer is yes. I'm here to help Damon take the Chalice from you and restore it to the priests of Zaire. So snooks to you!'

'Silence!' Adam wondered how many more times he was going to bellow out that word. But this time the Black Baron was literally shaking with anger, and he fought to control himself. 'Listen, all of you. I shall tell you this once and never again. The Chalice is MINE, by right of conquest, which is the only right I recognise, and it shall remain MINE for all time. And it is my intention to put you all to a death SO terrible that it will serve as a salutary warning and a deterrent to any others who may be so stupid as to wish to come to MY island and MY Castle to steal anything that is MINE.'

227

At that, the clean-shaven man in the green cloak rose to his feet.

'Sire, permit me to speak.'

The Black Baron gave him a cold look and then said, 'Speak if you must, Lord of the Treasury.'

'Sire, I plead for clemency for the prisoners. Four of them are but children, whilst the fifth is a servant, who cannot be held responsible for what he is ordered to do. Whatever their purpose in coming here, they have as yet done no harm...'

'No harm?' roared the Black Baron. 'They have trespassed on MY island, they have murdered many of MY guards, they have destroyed MY property, and they have insulted me ... ME, the Black Baron of Xakkara! Is THIS what you refer to as "no harm"?'

'As to your guards, most of them are robots and were thus not murdered,' said the Lord of the Treasury, pale now but clearly determined to pursue his defence of the prisoners. 'The destruction of property is minimal and they did not mean to insult you. I beg of you, in the name of mercy, let them go!'

The Black Baron looked at him with malice gleaming in his eyes.

'Let me get this straight, Lord of the Treasury,' he said, speaking softly but with immense malevolence. 'Do I understand that you dare to speak up on behalf of these criminals? They have all admitted their guilt, their iniquitous purpose in trespassing on my island and breaking into my castle, a purpose only thwarted by my cunning defences and my loyal guards. Do you, my Lord of the Treasury, dare to intercede on behalf of such villains? If so, I begin to wonder if you are indeed the right one to be my successor when the time is ripe.'

'Sire, they are not criminals, nor villains,' said the other stubbornly. 'Look at them! They are not evil. Misguided, perhaps, but not evil. In the name of goodness and forbearance, let them go.'

'Never!' bellowed the Black Baron. 'Die they must, and die they shall. This is MY wish and I am Master here. Or do you dare to dispute that also?'

'No sire,' said the other reluctantly. 'But...'

'Enough! Be seated, or I shall have you put to death alongside them.'

A man on the left of the Lord of the Treasury pulled him back down into his chair and whispered to him, and he nodded and remained seated. The Black Baron glared at him for a while, then turned his attention back to the prisoners.

'Look,' said Damon desperately. 'Let ME suffer this death of yours, not the others. They are blameless. Let them go. I will be your only victim.'

'No, Damon, no!' The exclamation exploded from Candice. Then she added, quietly, 'If you die, I die too. I don't think I want to live without you.'

Damon took her hand and squeezed it. 'Thanks, my love,' he said, much affected by her declaration. 'I won't forget this. As far as I'm concerned it's you and me from now on.'

Adam, to his own surprise, found himself so impressed by Candice's outburst that he said impulsively, 'All for one and one for all. Isn't that what you said, Damon? I'm with you in this.'

'And me, Adam!' cried Belle. 'I'll come with you, wherever you go.'

He squeezed her hand as the Black Baron nodded with evil satisfaction and then looked at Uno.

'And you, little minion. Would you not like to go free?'

'Master command me look after others,' replied Uno placidly. 'This I do. So I go with them.'

'Nice one, Uno!' said Damon.

'Silence!' The Black Baron looked at them coldly. 'So be it. You will then get your wish – you will all die together. And would you like to know how?' He gave a deep-throated humourless laugh. 'I am going to feed you to my Guardian!'

A loud mutter ran through the crowds in the Great Hall, composed partly of awe, partly of fear, and partly of some other reaction that, for some reason, made Adam feel that they were not all on their Master's side. The Lord of the Treasury may also have felt this, because he again rose to his feet.

'Sire, once again I plead for clemency for these prisoners. If the penalty you deem necessary is the ultimate one of death, then let it be a merciful one, swift and painless, and NOT the dreaded Guardian, I beg of you...'

'Silence, importunate dog!' shrieked the Black Baron. 'One more word of treason from you, insolent knave, and you shall join them! But more than that...' he added as the other opened his mouth to speak again '...your wife and children shall accompany you. Do you understand, dog?'

The Lord of the Treasury looked daggers at him, then shrugged and sat down again, this time without having to be persuaded.

'Don't worry, old son!' Damon called out to him. He looked at the Black Baron impudently. 'What's a rotten old Guardian to us, anyway? There are five of us to deal with him. All for one and one for all, that's our motto. We'll take on your Guardian and we'll win!'

'Brave talk!' sneered the Black Baron. 'However, it may interest you to know that, up to the present day, some thirty-seven fighters have tackled the Guardian in its lair – including a group of six all at once – and not ONE has survived. I merely tell you this to prevent you feeling over-confident.'

The five adventurers drew closer together and tried not to look too concerned.

'Enough talk,' said the Black Baron. 'But, since most of you are but children, I am going to give you one chance. You may take into the arena one weapon between the five of you. Now then, which shall it be? Knife ... cudgel ... spear ... axe? You may choose one of those four. Which shall it be?'

Damon looked at the others and was about to speak when Uno said, 'Master Adam had catapult, removed by guard. Request it be weapon.'

The Baron stared at him, then gestured to the leader of the guards.

'Bring the device mentioned to me,' he ordered.

'Yes sire,' said the man, who bowed low and withdrew. Meanwhile Uno was immediately surrounded by his exasperated companions (with the exception of Belle) who demanded, quite angrily, to know why he had said that: Damon adding that, in HIS opinion, of all the weapons named, the catapult would be the most useless. But Uno remained imperturbable, and refused to answer their heated remonstrations and criticisms. By then the leader of the guards had returned and now held up Adam's catapult for inspection. The Baron stared at it for a moment, then threw his head back

231

and laughed uproariously, many of his henchmen joining in. The outburst of laughter made Adam blush indignantly, but Uno continued to look impassive.

'THAT puny little thing!' said the Black Baron derisively, when he had recovered. 'You wouldn't rather settle for an axe or a spear? That ... that piece of rubbish wouldn't cause a sparrow a moment's worry!' He gave the leader of the guards a sharp look. 'You examined it to make sure it was harmless and had no magical properties?'

'I'd stake my life on it, sire – it is merely a child's toy,' said the leader confidently.

'Very well then,' said the Baron. He looked at Uno. 'You are quite sure you prefer this – this plaything? Make up your mind: once you choose, you will not have the opportunity to change your mind later.'

'Uno!' hissed Damon. 'Be sensible – take the axe or the spear. In fact, take anything but that useless object.'

Uno shook his furry head and gazed steadily at the Black Baron.

'Choose catapult,' he said calmly.

'Very well. Your wish is granted.' A cruel smile spread across the Baron's face. 'But you will remember that I did say only ONE weapon, did I not? And I am a man of my word. You will therefore be permitted to have only ONE stone for your catapult.' He laughed again, a cold, heartless laugh that sent shivers down the backs of the prisoners. Then he gestured to the leader. 'Take them away and prepare the arena for the sport to come.' His black eyes lingered on the captives. 'You will, I am sure, enjoy dying in front of an appreciative audience.'

His mocking laughter, echoed by others around the

table, followed them as they were hustled away from the Great Hall. As they went, Damon hissed to Uno, 'Now you've done it! What good is that ... that THING going to be against any kind of monster – especially with only one shot? You should have gone for one of the other weapons – we might have had a chance then.'

'Have chance now,' replied Uno serenely. 'Adam excellent shot.'

Damon was gloomily silent.

7

About an hour later the five prisoners were released from the small dungeon in which they had been incarcerated since receiving their death sentence. All were unarmed, save for Adam, who had his catapult and one sharp, flint-like stone about the size of a large hen's egg. Despite Uno's optimism, the others had expressed serious doubts about the adequacy of such a weapon against any foe – and Adam, although remaining diplomatically silent, had felt inclined to agree. But the die was now cast.

The leader of the guards had wanted to take Custard from them, but Candice had put up such a fierce opposition to the move that in the end she had been allowed to carry the dog with her. Their collective hearts beat faster, and their mouths were dry, as they were led down a stone passage, through a pair of iron gates set in a high archway, and out into a wide open space with Castle buildings on all sides. The stone walls towered up into the blue sky and they could feel the warmth of the sun on their faces.

On two sides of the open space, behind the security of iron bars, there were stands decorated with coloured cloths and bunting, with people seated in them. One of them was occupied by the lower orders: a motley selection of guards, servants, huntsmen, wenches, musicians and serfs all bunched together on rough

234

wooden benches. On the other side was the stand clearly reserved for the top people: the ruling classes, the noblemen, the stewards, the high-born ladies in their finery and jewels, all seated on cushioned seats with ample elbow-room. And in the centre of the front row sat the Black Baron, with his female companions on either side. In front of him, on a pedestal, stood a black box.

At the far end of the open space there was, built into solid rock, a huge dark cage; the thick iron bars at the front must have measured ten metres in height and width. There was enough light from the arena percolating into the dark depths of the cage for the prisoners to see a huge metal shutter right at the rear of the cage, covering – what? As the five companions were herded into the centre of the space, and felt sand beneath their feet, Damon uttered a loud exclamation.

'By thunder! It IS an arena and we're the performing troupe, due to take part in a fight to the death in front of all these people, and we don't even know who or what our opponent is going to be.'

'Silence!' roared the leader of the guards, taking a leaf from the Black Baron's book. He waited until the five were silent, then he wheeled to face the Black Baron, and bowed low. 'The prisoners are all present and correct, sire.'

'Very well. Dismiss!'

The escorting guards and their leader clumped off through the archway, and the iron gates clanged shut behind then; an iron bar was slid across through iron sockets, closing the gates so that those inside the open space could not escape. The five were left standing in the middle of the arena under the warm sunshine, a

235

small, lonely group huddled together, watched by countless eyes and jeered at by rough tongues.

'I didn't much like the sound of those gates closing,' complained Candice. 'It was a bit too doom-laden for my liking.' She hugged the quivering body of the dog to her. 'How did I get into this? All I did was offer to guide these two children to Castroglio's abode and now look where I am! What have I ever done to deserve this?'

'I AM sorry I got you into all this, Candice,' said Belle contritely.

'I'm not blaming you, kiddo. Nor you, Adam. I'm blaming no one but myself. I made the decision, so I take the consequences. And in a way I'm half-glad I did, because otherwise I'd never have met you, Damon – and the rest of you lot.' She looked round at them and grinned faintly. 'Now I come to think of it, I wouldn't have missed it for worlds!'

'I could wish we'd met under happier circumstances,' said Damon. 'You're really my style, you know?' He squeezed her hand. 'But don't you worry – we'll see it through.'

'We've had some good times together,' said Adam, more to keep their spirits up than for any other reason. 'Right, Belle?'

'Yes, Adam. We quarrelled a bit at the beginning, but not for long. And not any more...'

'Oh yes you will,' asserted Damon. 'You'll quarrel again, lots of times. That's half the fun. And be sure that we're all going to live through this. No fight is ever lost before it's over. Eh, Uno?'

'Wise saying,' nodded the dwarf, still as placid as ever. 'But must not underestimate unknown opponent. Must prepare for worst.'

'Silence!' roared the Black Baron for the umpteenth time. 'Enough of this useless chatter. Pay attention! You will observe this box in front of me. It contains that priceless object which you covet, and which – you may be sure – will never fall into your hands. Behold – the Chalice!'

One of the Baron's retainers lifted the box and opened it. There was a sudden flash of sunlight striking gold, awakening the bright sparkle of light reflected from many-faceted jewels. They saw, on a pedestal, a goblet such as they had never seen before. It was perfectly-shaped, the epitome of delicate form, made from pure gold, with two gently-curving symmetrical handles. And it was studded with rare gems of almost every kind – amethysts, carnelians, opals, garnets, turquoises, agates, beryls, zircons, moonstones, aquamarines, onyx, sardonyx and tourmalines.

'The Chalice of Saint Anthony,' said the Baron impressively. 'MY Chalice. I caused all those precious stones to be added to it. Before that it was just a golden goblet, valuable but not priceless. Now it is beyond price, beyond value – and it is ALL mine. I have allowed you to see it now, because you will never see it again. It is mine, and it will remain mine for all time. Replace it in the box.'

The retainer obeyed him, and the glitter and sparkle of the treasure of treasures disappeared once more. The Baron fixed them with his cruel mocking eyes.

'And now! Prepare for your blood to freeze in your veins, your hearts to stop beating, your hopes to die. For you are about to meet the Guardian of the Chalice.'

He gave a sign. For a long, breathless moment nothing happened. Even the assembled audience ceased

237

momentarily to jeer and murmur and guffaw, and an ominous silence blanketed the arena. Then, at the far end, another rumble issued from the cage and the shutter at the rear slowly rose up and up, until it too disappeared.

And from the foetid darkness that had lain behind the shutter there billowed into the cage an entity so vast and so horrendously hideous that the five prisoners were struck dumb and paralysed with terror. From the audience, who presumably had seen it before, came a long-drawn-out sigh of shuddering fear.

Its gigantic bulk filled the cage. Adam's starting eyes and chaotically-churning brain formed an impression of an incredibly interwoven tangle of thick coiled tentacles, all at least a metre in girth, immensely strong, and covered with a dense growth of bristly, grey-brown hair, all of which were squirming and writhing and meshing and coiling in slow motion. From various parts of the titanic and constantly-writhing confusion of coils projected eight or more long necks with, at the end of each one, a huge spiky head with facial lineaments so ugly and so diabolical that they beggared description. Every now and then, from the central aperture in each set of features, a long, red prehensile, sting-like member darted out with lightning speed, and from the same orifices issued green vapour with a stench so strong and so repulsive that the five hapless victims were already gasping and retching.

Candice found her voice first.

'Oh great whistling warthogs!' she said faintly. 'We're done for.'

They heard the Black Baron laugh loudly and they saw him stand up and point to the monster. 'Behold

238

– the Guardian!' he said in a voice full of evil triumph. 'Behold it – and DIE!'

He gave another sign and the iron bars between the bestial monstrosity and the prisoners rumbled upwards into the roof of the cage. Its gargantuan occupant gave vent to a series of awesome gurgling roars, and undulated out of the cage into the sunlight, its vast entanglement of tentacles gleaming with foul slime, coiling, uncoiling, writhing and wriggling like a dense mesh of thick fleshy wool, and its lethal-looking stings erupting from the evil fissures in its many heads as each 'face' turned bulbous glassy eyes on the huddle of victims. The gigantic entity, at least as big as a house, got into motion and lumbered towards them with slow deliberation, propelled (as far as they could see) by the squirming movement of its lower tentacles rather than by any other means.

The companions backed away, white-faced and shivering with a mixture of primeval fear and complete repulsion.

'You fool, Uno!' said Damon in a hoarse voice. 'The catapult's going to be totally USELESS against that – utterly useless.'

'Axe or spear no better,' replied Uno, seemingly as calm as ever.

'Uno, try your powder, please!' gasped Adam.

'Yes, yes, do it, Uno!' exclaimed Candice.

'Not much left. May not work. Not sure...'

'Use it, use it, PLEASE!' screamed Belle.

Uno shrugged and, as the enormous, squirming behemoth billowed nearer to them, and they were sickened afresh by the stench, the furry dwarf opened his little purse, emptied the remainder of the white powder into his paw, threw it into the air and said aloud a number of untranslatable words and syllables.

Then they waited, breathless with trepidation.

But nothing happened.

The writhing, coiling monster did not disappear. It remained unharmed and solidly visible, horrific in its size, in its proximity, in its abhorrent and paralysing menace.

'No use,' said Uno.

'It ... it didn't work!' gasped Damon.

'No good, no good at all!' moaned Adam.

'We're ... we're done for!' whispered Belle, half-fainting with terror.

'Useless!' said Candice between her teeth. 'Now what can we do?'

'Prepare catapult,' instructed Uno.

The others stared at him with incredulity and anger.

'Prepare catapult?' repeated Damon, stupefied. 'What good will that do, for goodness' sake?'

'Not for goodness' sake,' answered Uno calmly. 'For our sake.'

'It ... it won't do ANY good against that ... that thing!' moaned Adam.

'Nevertheless, prepare catapult,' responded Uno.

Adam shrugged and took the stone from his pocket and fitted it into the pouch of his catapult. Meanwhile, from the monster's many mouths issued roars of fury and it billowed towards them again, the long narrow necks reaching down to enable the tongues to lash out at the shrinking five. It displayed a surprising turn of speed and, when Adam tried to dodge round it, a head snaked down, a long sting darted out, and he was forced to retreat back to where the others crouched.

240

Once again they were compelled to back away and soon they were hard against the iron gates, with nowhere else to go. Candice rattled the gates, to no good purpose, and they thought they heard a mocking laugh from the Black Baron. The titan monstrosity lumbered towards them again then paused about five metres from them, the weaving necks and darting tongues effectively cutting off any possible chance of escape. Candice stopped, still clutching Custard, snatched up a handful of sand and flung it at the nearest head, but it had no effect other than to make the mammoth's many mouths roar again and the many heads lower themselves on their long necks towards the victims.

'This is it,' Adam said bleakly. 'There's nothing we can do.'

'Isn't there?' shouted Damon. 'Well, I for one don't intend to go down without a fight. Who's with me?'

He set his jaw firmly and started forward towards the huge bulk of the squirming mass. Uno caught at his arm.

'No good. You die. Better way. Remember poem.'

'Poem?' Damon said blankly, looking at him as though he had gone mad. 'What are you babbling about? What poem?'

'You mean the one the old man gave us?' asked Candice alertly.

'Yes. Remember what said?' Uno, apparently oblivious of the slavering behemoth looming menacingly over them, quoted:

'When the dreamer awakes
Then dies his dream
When the pale moon sets

Then fades its beam
So muffle the church bells
No more will they chime
And kill off the poet
No more will he rhyme.'

He turned to Adam. 'Use catapult quickly pliss.'

Adam levelled the loaded catapult at the monster.
'But ... which part shall I aim at?' he asked, bewildered.

'Not at monster. At Baron. Middle of forehead. Shoot
now!'

Adam stared at him in amazement for a split second,
but just then the giant entity's heads roared in unison
and reached out for the five companions. Adam
swivelled, aimed between the iron bars in front of the
stand at the Black Baron's forehead and let fly.

It was without any doubt the best shot he'd ever
made in his short life. He had never before been so
accurate, and would probably never be again. But on
this one occasion the stone flew from the catapult
straight and true, and as fast as an arrow, to its target.
The Black Baron reared upright, clutched at his forehead,
uttered a choking, bellowing scream, and then fell
forward against the protective bars – which, of course,
had done him no good at all.

And at the same moment as the Baron died, within
the arena there was a strange, indescribable 'bursting'
sound and, in full view of the astounded eyes of the
five companions and the incredulous gaze of the
audience, the towering, squirming, writhing monster
completely disappeared.

8

The five stood totally stunned, whilst the audience seemed to be equally shocked by what had happened. It was Damon who first recovered his senses.

'We've done it!' he breathed. Then he yelled 'WE'VE DONE IT! The Guardian is dead!'

They pranced with joy, hugging one another in delirious pleasure and relief. Custard joined in with excited yelps and Candice could not resist kissing him on his wet nose.

'Good old Adam!' shouted Damon. 'What a fantastic shot!'

'I grant you that, but I only did what Uno told me,' said Adam, still dazed by the sudden and shocking turn of events. 'Why, Uno? I don't understand.'

'I do,' said Candice. 'The poem was a clue. If someone creates an illusion, and the creator dies, then the illusion dies with him. The Black Baron had, by the use of his magical powers, created the Guardian to protect the Chalice. It was not real and, when the Baron died, it died as well.'

'In that case why didn't the powder work?' asked Belle.

'Not enough left,' said Uno. 'Guardian too big. But we win – thanks to Master Adam.'

'No, no,' said Adam quickly. 'Thanks to YOU, Uno.'

'And Damon!' added Candice. 'We couldn't have got through without him.'

'And you girls,' said Damon. 'You helped a great deal.'

'Many self-congratulations in order,' said Uno calmly. 'But word of warning. Not have Chalice yet, and not escaped yet.'

Thus brought back to stern reality, they turned to face the audience, prepared to fight on. But they stared in blank amazement as they saw all the audience – guards, servants, musicians, wenches, serfs – and even the ruling classes, the nobles, lords and ladies – leaping about, cheering and singing and dancing with joy, kissing one another with happiness, just as they themselves had done.

'What's happened?' gasped Damon.

One of the lords stood up on a bench. He had discarded his cloak, but they saw at once that it was the Lord of the Treasury again in the limelight.

'Listen, everyone!' he shouted. 'The Black Baron is dead! The long years of tyranny are over. The Baron, his dreaded Guardian and his diabolical sorcery, are no more! Now, at long last, peace and goodwill can return to this realm. I, the Lord of the Treasury, swear on my honour that this will be so.'

The rest of his speech was lost in a burst of renewed cheering and applause, and more hugging and dancing. He waited, smiling indulgently, until it had subsided, then held up his hands for silence.

'And we owe our deliverance to those five good people in the arena,' he shouted. 'But for them we should still be under the yoke of foul repression. Let us give them their reward! Let us immediately prepare a great feast of thanksgiving, and invite them along as guests of honour. And, as a final demonstration of our

244

regret and remorse at the way they have been treated, let us give them the Chalice, so that they may fulfil their quest and return it in triumph to the rightful owners!'

These suggestions were greeted with acclamation and a tremendous outburst of enthusiasm and more cheering. The bars were removed and the people swarmed across the arena, lifted the five still-dazed adventurers onto their shoulders and carried them round the open space in a grand procession of triumph, Custard joining in with wildly-excited yelps.

When things had calmed down, and the Great Hall was being prepared and bedecked for the feast, the five were presented to the Lord of the Treasury, and Adam at last had a chance to talk to him. When he revealed who he was, and why he had made the long and arduous journey to the Castle, the man was deeply amazed and very interested. He put his arm round Adam's shoulder.

'My boy, you need have no more worries,' he said. 'Your quest is over. It is well known that our late and unlamented ruler, the Black Baron, arranged that infamous attack on the Moldavian Palace in order to appropriate the Chalice for himself. It is also well-known, within these walls at least, that there was NO inside assistance for any member of the Palace staff. On the contrary, the name of your father is written in the documents as one who defended the museum and its treasure with great courage and skill. His death was a truly sad occurrence. But cheer up! I shall personally arrange to have a statement prepared, in writing, not only exonerating your father from any blame but also praising him for his valour and for his integrity, and

I shall sign it myself. Now, my boy, will that do for you?'

Adam was unable to reply – he was choked by this sudden and total realisation of his dreams. But eventually he stammered his thanks, and the Lord of the Treasury laughed heartily and slapped him on the back and left him to the congratulations of his four companions, and – once again – the excited yelping of Custard.

Later that evening, at the feast of thanksgiving in the Great Hall, the five were royally wined and dined, and there were numerous speeches from all sorts of people: and Damon made a brief but suitable reply on behalf of the five adventurers. Then came the presentation. The Lord of the Treasury, richly attired in red velvet and wearing a purple cloak trimmed with ermine, stood up. There was a roll on the drums from the musicians, who had been put up in the gallery, and a sober silence descended on the assembly.

'Ladies and gentlemen, lords and ladies, friends and comrades,' he said. 'The long, dark days of the Black Baron's oppression are ended. He kept the unfortunate people of this realm enslaved and suppressed by fearful wizardry and by his evil will, and in particular by his monstrous creation of the dreaded Guardian. Now he is dead! No more will the mere mention of the Guardian spread terror throughout the land; no more will the honest people of this realm be cowed and subjugated by his diabolical trickery. Now we can get down to work to rebuild our land, and our future, and in particular to make peace with the other inhabitants of this Island, so that we may all live together in amity and goodwill.'

He paused for the consequent storm of applause and acclamation to die down.

246

'And now,' he resumed, 'I have the very greatest pleasure in making not one but TWO presentations.' He held up an impressive scroll, plentifully adorned with red sealing wax and blue ribbons. 'This is a signed declaration that Sector-Captain Adam Arrowsmith, of the Palace Guard of Moldavia, behaved with conspicuous gallantry and courage, and acquitted himself with all honour, on the occasion of the infamous attack by the depraved forces of the Black Baron on the Museum. It also states that equal distinction and honour accrues to his son Adam, who travelled far, and dared much, to vindicate his father's reputation.'

Amid cheers, a blushing Adam took charge of his scroll, and when he returned to his seat, Damon and Uno shook his hand, Candice and Belle kissed his cheeks (one each), and Custard licked all over his face with wet affection.

'And now,' said the Lord of the Treasury, 'I would like to make a second presentation, this time to the young man named Damon, who is truly representative of all these plucky youngsters and their small but honourable friend Uno. I wish to present to him this precious Chalice – the Sacred Chalice of St Anthony – with our heartfelt gratitude and best wishes, in recognition of the great debt we owe to him and his friends, in the knowledge that he will faithfully restore it to the rightful owners, The High Priests of Zaire, thus putting right the terrible wrong that has been done for so many years.'

Damon rose and walked over to the speaker and took from his hands the fabulous Chalice of St Anthony. With a grin of sheer unadulterated pleasure he raised the trophy high above his head.

'We've got it!' he shouted.

Two days later the five adventurers, together with Custard the dog, *and* the Chalice (wrapped in cloth to disguise it), *and* Adam's precious scroll, left the Castle on their way firstly to Castroglio's abode to drop Uno, and then home for the remainder of the party, after which Damon would then set out for the distant Realm of Zaire to hand over the Chalice to the High Priests thereof.

They were escorted across the island by a group of soldiers (real friendly soldiers, *not* robots) and were delighted to find the *Kingfisher* just where they had left her. They swiftly embarked and set sail, waving goodbye to their escorts as the little boat headed out to sea.

Later that same day, a violent storm blew up unexpectedly and their little boat was assailed by the incredible fury of the raging elements, blown right off its true course, and...

But that's another story.